Written by
TERESA LEE

Leggins

Illustrated by
JANN JOHNSON LARDIE

Produced by:

FriesenPress

Suite 300 – 990 Fort Street
Victoria, BC, Canada V8V 3K2

www.friesenpress.com

Distributed to the trade by The Ingram Book Company

Dedication

This book is dedicated to my mother, Audrey Cole, one of my best friends. Thanks Mamma, for always being there. I could never adequately express my appreciation for the blessing of having you as a mother. TL

* * *

I dedicate my artistic efforts in Leggins to "Mrs. Larkin," a special character in this book. "Mrs. Larkin" is a very real and wonderful person, Joann Lardie, whom I've been blessed to call "Mom" for nearly 45 years. As a remarkable teacher, she touched and inspired many lives. However, to me, she is the very best Mother-in-Law a bride could have! Thanks, Mom for supporting me in all I do – and, for sharing Bump with me. JJL

* * *

This book is also dedicated to best friends everywhere. May the friendship stories, that each person holds with-in their own heart, bring a smile in the remembering.

Acknowledgments

Bringing a book through the process of putting pen to paper (or more recently keyboard to text document) with the intent of publication, takes much effort and dedication on the part of many people. A good writer involves multiple pools of talent in the journey. These joint efforts provide a diverse network of support, criticism, ideas for revision, brain-storming, and feedback. With that said, I have some treasured people that deserve recognition and praise for their efforts and assistance in the accomplishment of Leggins.

Jann Johnson Lardie, my dear friend, accomplished artist and now illustrator has spent endless hours laboring over the designs that she has incorporated into the book to help make it interesting and informative for the reader. She works hard to get her illustrations precise, with research and detail that captures setting and character. I could never thank her enough for her patience as a dear friend, and for her unwavering support along the way as we collaborated. Leggins is our second book accomplished together. Also worthy of mention, is the way that she encourages others to follow their dreams. Many new artists, in a range of medium expression, have benefited from her counsel and example.

Gratefulness beyond measure goes to my very talented colleagues and readers in critical revision, for editing of text and helpful suggestions regarding writer's craft: Jann Johnson Lardie, Bernadette Leone, Debra Mercer, and Ann Williams. Thanks also to Brandon Lardie for his technical savvy and Keely Schanski for generously providing necessary photos.

I cannot be remiss in also mentioning some of my very dear fourth and fifth grade friends at Murphy Elementary in Haslett, Michigan: The students in Mrs. Rios' fifth grade class and Mrs. Moore's fourth grade class (2013-2014). Their honest critiquing helped me enormously. Their incredible feedback and specific suggestions offered for revision helped improve the story on several levels. These young friends, remarkably savvy readers, offered up valuable ideas that helped create the book presented here.

Eternal thanks is offered to my extensive and most precious family for their continuing support and encouragement on the three-year-journey we all traveled to publication of both my books. Especially to my dear husband, for tolerating my obsession, and displaying incredible patience, as I reinvented myself into a writer... the dream I have always envisioned.

Last but not least, my continued gratefulness to FriesenPress, for all the help along the way and the solid safety net provided me as a new author. I could never fully express the comfort that Friesen's entire staff presents in their cordial attitudes and genuine concern for me as an author. Ever since the initial signing of my first book, Boxcar Joe, I have experienced only the most courteous and respectful relationship. Thank you for respecting the dignity of all struggling writers.

Table of Contents

Best friends come in all shapes
and sizes, colors and cultures.
They come with different interests and gifts.

Friendship treasures can be
found within families,
or discovered in a chance meeting
between complete strangers.

Whatever **your** story may be,
honor it, share it, cherish it, forever.
Unconditional love is sometimes
a once-in-a-lifetime blessing.

Author's Reflections

This is the story of Leggins and Mary Francis. It is our story and more. It tells of fun with family and friends. It explores some of the agonies we all experience on our journey through life. Most of all it recalls lessons we eventually manage to learn about the true meaning of sharing ourselves with others.

Find parts of yourself in this story and remember that everything lasts but a short time. Take comfort that memories, of earlier days filled with friendship and fun, can bring it all flooding back anytime you wish to enter the remembering. Trust that genuine friendships last forever. Know in your heart that sometimes the first ones are the best friendship treasures of all. Just ask me or Mary Francis.

Throughout the story, I allow you a peek into my inner most thoughts and feelings. I share those with you throughout the book; recorded in the *italicized print* at the beginning of chapters. Those segments share with the reader reactions I have to story situations, sometimes imbedded within the body of paragraphs, and in pre/post appendices of the book. My hope is that through these personal revelations of heart and mind, you will come to know the author not only as the storyteller, but as a friend you once met in a book you read.

Come along with me and Mary Francis as we travel the road to growing-up and along the way find a treasure that is priceless. TL

Chapter One

No Safety in Nicknames

Mary Francis and I knew for sure that grown-ups seemed to know about friendship stuff. My daddy fought in World War II, and once told us, "Best friends have each other's back." He went on to explain, "You can trust that person to protect you from others who might try to hurt you. They want what's best for you. A best friend doesn't suggest doing things that might harm you. In fact, a true friend protects you from harm."

Leggins, that's me. At home I usually answer to Terry (yep, spelled like the boys' name) *or* Teresa Lee when I'm in big trouble. Mary Francis Carson, my best friend, got stuck with a boys' name, too. Her middle name came from her dad, who got his middle name from his dad. It always made her hoppin' mad that they slapped a boys' name on her and there wasn't one thing to be done about it! She and I figured out that it must have been destiny for both of us to have had the same misfortune of carrying around a name usually attached to the opposite gender. Lucky for us we were best friends. Together it would be easier enduring a nuisance like that. Having boys' names was only one reason why we stuck to each other like glue.

You might be wondering where the name of Leggins came from? Well, Leggins is a nickname that I got stuck with, on account of the woolen snow pants that Mamma insisted that I wear. Whenever the crispness of the autumn air turned to snowflakes or the temperature fell below forty degrees, she pulled out those woolen leggings to help keep me warm through the long Michigan winters. Mamma was no nonsense on that issue.

The older fifth grade safety patrol boys liked to tease me relentlessly about those dull gray, patched pants that always covered my legs and showed below the dresses that I wore to school. Almost every day of the week during the cold season, you could see me wearing those dreaded things! So, the name they invented just seemed to stick and it was "Leggins," this and "Leggins" that for every day of school spent at Robert Kerr Elementary. Even when the weather was warm and snow pants were not part of my daily attire, I carried the name like a flea on a dog. It irritated me to no end, but never went away. No matter how much I scratched, clawed, or complained it just wouldn't stop bothering.

The older safety patrol boys from Robert Kerr School were always waiting and watching from their post at the corner of Cambridge and Monroe Rd. The predictable turn up the block on my way to school was their signal to start in on me.

"Hey, Leggins!" would begin the daily banter of shouting out my nickname for everyone to hear. They always cared for my safety, just not so much for my feelings.

They'd continue with great relish, "Hey, Leggins! Here comes Leggins!"

"Leggins is laggin' and her coat-tails is draggin'! Hurry- up, Leggins! *You're* late for school!" Even when I wasn't!

I never understood why "Leggins" was such a delight for them to yell day in and day out. Sometimes it brought tears to my eyes when I was overly tired or not feeling too well. That always made Mary Francis hopping mad, and no one wanted to get her riled up! When Mary Francis was steaming mad, her dark eyes snapped a warning, and those pesky boys would stop their teasing immediately. They didn't want one of her tantrums getting them expelled from their safety crossing post. They liked being on safety patrol because that job kept them out of class a little longer at the start of each school day.

Even Dale Hensley (*more on him later*) protected me once from their teasing. He let Curtis Evans, one of the substitute safeties, have it smack dab in the chops for calling me, "A gray peanut from the wrong side of the tracks." I was the smallest girl in my class, so I got the peanut part. But really, what was the big deal? When the weather turned cold every little girl, who wore dresses to school, had on leggings underneath. Sometimes we just tucked our dress skirts inside our snow pants, which was the very reason those pants made us look fat. Wearing woolen leggings to school had nothing, whatsoever, to do with what side of the tracks you came from.

Mary Francis and I had more than one fight with pesky boys over "Leggins". The most memorable scrape over my nickname got Tommy Trundle expelled from safety patrol for one whole month and grounded for two weeks by his parents. Afterward, Mary Francis carried her black eye around like a badge of honor and announced her intentions toward anyone who so much as thought about calling me " Leggins Fat Pants", in her presence. I admit that I did feel awfully bad about my best friend getting a black eye on my account.

It was nearing the end of January with snow piled high everywhere. The snow plows had caused huge snow banks along the sidewalks to tower like walled forts lining the street side. For nearly a week, neighborhood moms took turns walking their kids back and forth to Robert Kerr School. They harped about being careful, as most moms do. All along the way, the talk was about the safety rules for walking when cars couldn't see walkers over the mountains of snow. Five long days, of making the three block hike with a parent and having to repeat (at least twenty times) "S-T-O-P at E-S-C" (that was short for Every Single Corner). *We got it! How could we not get it?* They were finally satisfied and discontinued the daily trek; much to the relief of every school-aged kid on the block.

The day started out bright and beautiful, with the sky as blue and dazzling as we had seen it in weeks, and the sun shining as if it would never quit. Not one cloud anywhere in sight. Seven of the neighborhood regulars, including me and Mary Francis, were walking to school along our street, Dartmouth Drive. It was now a tunneled but familiar path with walls of snow on either side that we couldn't see over. No parents today, but still we were responsible and stopped at each corner. After-all, we had carefully practiced for the better part of one whole week. The cars couldn't see us until we were right at the crossing. We remembered the rule.

Just to be funny that day, we decided to repeat loudly and with a twist, the familiar phrase we had recited for over a week. All for the sake of being able to laugh at the end of saying it. Tromping along in our boots, all seven of us shouted out loudly, "S-T-O-P and

TERESA LEE

S-O-T," (that's short for Stop and Stick-Out-Tongue). Of course we did just that, to each other, and then laughed our heads off!

We were zipped, buttoned, tied, and bundled up against the snow and cold. All of us were in a happy mood over the sunny day that had greeted us that crisp morning. After three blocks of shouting and laughing our safety slogan all along the way, we reached the corner of Cambridge Drive and Monroe Road. Here we usually crossed over to the school-yard which was located directly on the opposite side of the paved road. Four, fifth grade Safeties suddenly appeared around the end of the sky-high snow drifts that opened up to the crosswalk.

Tommy Trundle just happened to be on duty this morning because Danny Sheaver was sick with the flu. At least that was the story they gave us. Tommy had a reputation for being loud-mouthed and bossy, especially when he was surrounded by other boys his age who were bigger than him, which was usually most of the time. Mary Francis and I agreed that Tommy Trundle spent a good share of his time trying to make up for his smaller size by shooting off his mouth, when he probably shouldn't. He was not to disappoint today. Sure enough, he started right in.

"Well, if it ain't the Dartmouth Dunces! With Miss Leggins, Fat Pants herself leading this sorry sight," he sneered. "What's the racket about anyway? We've been listening to that kindygarden baby blab for the last two blocks you've walked! Oh yes, it's 'S-T-O-P at ESC'," he mimicked in a baby like voice. "I hear tell you've been at that chant for almost a week now! Who taught you that stupid nursery rhyme? What does it mean anyway?" he finished with scornful demand. My eyes started to fill with tears at his stinging words.

"Well today it's S-T-O-P and S-O-T!" Dale shot back as both Nelson brothers, in unison, stuck out their tongues at Tommy. All seven of the "Dartmouth Dunces" laughed. However, with Tommy not so much!

"Mighty funny boys aren't you? Want to make something of it?" Tommy snarled.

"Shut up, Mr. Tommy T. Pip-Squeak or you just might be eating snow for breakfast!" Mary Francis raged right back.

"Well, Miss Mary Francis Mind Your Own Business **who** exactly is going to serve it up on a plate? **Babies** can't cook!" he finished with a big grin. A show for the benefit of the gathering crowd of kids, just arriving at the corner on their walk to school.

"NO! But **girls** can!" Mary Francis countered. Then, without so much as a blink of her eyelash, she plowed head first into him with her arms locked stiffly in front of her for the powerful shove she delivered. It caught Tommy completely off guard, and he went down hard on the ice. Mary Francis wasted no time and jumped right on top of his stomach with a leg on either side, straddling Tommy Trundle in one swoop, scooping up snow as she went. Tommy swung a fist and hit Mary Francis squarely in the right eye, as the first handful of snow was shoved straight into his mouth. Mary never missed a beat! She never let up! Scoop, smash! Scoop, smash! Snow pushed forcefully in his face, up his nose, in his mouth over and over until Tommy was groaning for rescue. That was the signal for his safety patrol buddies to get Mary off from him and now! The other six of us, 'Dartmouth Dunces', stood frozen to the spot, not daring to move, fully expecting a free for all snowball fight or worse to begin momentarily as we stood our ground.

The surrounding speechless audience was stunned when two of the fifth grade safeties started laughing, as they dragged Mary Francis kicking and screaming off from Tommy.

"Oh boy, Tommy... you just got whupped by a girl!" they all cackled.

"How did you let that happen, being a big Safety and all?" Crowed Lenny Shots, the fifth grade safety captain.

"Who's the dunce now?" Aaron Farnick, another safety, snickered. Tommy jumped up ready to let the fists fly. Two of the other safeties held Tommy's arms, stopping him from doing further damage. All spectators took a few steps back.

Mary Francis was standing several feet away after having been yanked from the fight. She stood to the side brushing the snow off from her coat and mittens. Her right eye was red and swollen. Her eyelid was puffed out over her eyelashes so that you couldn't see them at all. Her eye was swollen shut to the point that it looked like the slice of a new moon in the night sky. With her coat torn slightly at the shoulder and the condition of her eye, she looked like some prize fighter after the final bell. So intent on the face washing that she was doling out to Tommy Trundle, she never shed a single tear, or even took notice of the punch to her eye or the rip in her coat. Mary Francis scooped up a mitten-full of snow and held it gingerly to her eye. *Still not a tear!* I was amazed at her brave and fearless response, but I shouldn't have been. I had seen her in this mode before. She was merciless in her revenge.

Tommy ceased his struggling and stood rubbing the bleeding scratches on his face. Some of the handfuls of snow had been mixed with slivers of ice. Each swipe from Mary Francis gouged his skin. Blood smeared his bottom lip and left cheek. I thought that I saw tears in his eyes, but he had been so mean, and such a bully, that I didn't feel one bit bad at his discomfort. *He deserved just what he got!*

"You Dartmouth Dunces are gonna' get yours!" Tommy threatened loudly.

"Yah? With what army? You just got beat up by a girl!" Denny Nelson sassed back bravely.

Kids, standing nearby watching the whole thing, started to laugh. Tommy lunged at the Nelson brothers to make good on his threat, but his fifth grade safety captors kept him from further trouble.

Mrs. Kurski or Mrs. K., our principal, seeing the fight from her office window which faced Monroe Street, promptly arrived on the scene. She immediately ordered to her office, all four of the fifth grade safety patrol boys standing there, including... Tommy Trundle.

Before dismissing anyone, she turned to the seven of us and said in a very precise manner, "S-T-O-P and cross the road safely. Mary Francis, I will speak with you later."

"Yes, Ma'am," Mary Francis quietly replied.

Tommy Trundle hung his head as he crossed the road behind the other safeties, all of them on the way to Mrs. Kurski's office.

Everyone left behind stood there watching the backs of the school principal and half of the fifth grade safeties trudge into the school. We were speechless. No one said a word for close to a minute. We rolled our wide-open eyes at each other, and then all attention went immediately to Mary Francis. Her battered eye was turning quickly into a ghastly bluish-black shade, despite the scoop of snow that she had used as a make-shift icepack. Mary Francis brushed her mittens together, back and forth several times, like she had just finished a very big job assigned to her.

She pointed directly at her battle worn eye, and proudly proclaimed, "Well, that Tommy T. got his breakfast and a little more! Hope he enjoyed every bite, 'cuz I sure enjoyed serving it up!"

"You can be on my team any day, Mary Francis." Dale offered kindly.

"Yep, never saw a girl take down a boy that fast before," Denny smiled.

I felt proud that she was my best friend. We walked arm in arm all the rest of the way to school.

Both Mary Francis and Tommy paid a visit to the school nurse that morning, but not at the same time. Mary Francis came back to our classroom with a bag of ice held to her eye. Tommy had a fat lip, and a Band-Aid on his left cheek, just below his eye.

Mary Francis got a stern lecture from Mrs. K. about fighting. Our principal had heard what a big bully Tommy had been from the other safeties and the crowd of kids standing near-by. She was clearly not seeing his side of things, so Mary Francis got off the hook easy with only a goodwill bargain, made with Mrs. K, for no more fighting.

Tommy on the other hand did not. He got suspended from safety patrol for a whole month. When he got home from school that day, his mom and dad were plenty mad at him! Mr. Carson and Mr. Trundle had a long, quiet conversation on the phone that evening. Mary Francis gladly shared that information, but not many details, since she was made to sit on her bed for over an hour for fighting in the first place. The next day at the corner crossing, Lenny Shots eagerly filled us in on how it went for Tommy. Two weeks of being grounded was not going to help improve the mood of Tommy T.!

What was the very best part for me? The daily teasing at the crossing stopped, at least for a while. It was a known fact: Mary Francis Carson was the bravest and best friend any girl could have. *She had my back. How could I be so lucky?!*

Chapter Two

As Neighborhoods Go...

When it came to Mary Francis and me, it took us a while to learn to appreciate each other. We were thrown together with no choice in the matter. My family moved into a brand new house that my daddy had built, right next door to Mary Francis and her family. We were both five years old, standing toe to toe, just across the property line. We had to make the best of it, with Mary Francis usually saying, "Yes, let's!" and me saying back, "No, we better not!" Things weren't always easy, but somehow our friendship managed to work out very well. I suppose that everyone could see the special twinkle we had when we were together, most especially when we were getting along, which was most of the time. After all, we had to "have each other's backs" living together in a neighborhood that was overpopulated with pesky boys!

Making friends is always the biggest issue with moving to a new place. Starting a friendship with someone new seems to be easier when you are younger. Our new neighborhood was full of kids, which we thought was a plus right off. Two families with kids lived just across the street. The Scotts lived, three doors down, across the street. They had two boys, Allen, the youngest and Mickey, the oldest. The Frelunds lived directly across the street from our house with two kids.

Mrs. Frelund was sister to Dale and Denny Nelson's mom. Their family lived just across the open field from Mary Francis' front porch. With the Nelson family living in the very next block, Mrs. Nelson and Mrs. Frelund only had to walk across the street to have coffee together. Mamma thought that was ever so nice, especially since she didn't have a sister that could be a best friend. The Frelund family had two kids: Mike, a boy near my age, and his much older teenaged sister who never played with us at all.

Dee-Dee Frelund was the neighborhood babysitter on many evenings when parents wanted a night out. She had a boyfriend named Wes, which was short for Wesley. He rode a black shiny motorcycle that was very loud. The neighborhood boys always ran over to Frelunds' whenever Wes came by. If he wasn't in a big hurry, he would let them take turns sitting on the bike seat, pretending to drive it. We all thought Wesley was a cool guy! He thought Dee-Dee Frelund was even cooler all dressed up to go out, with her long dark pony-tail and gray flannel poodle skirt. All the neighbor kids including Mike, Dee-Dee's brother, thought it unfortunate that Wes wasn't allowed to ride his motorcycle when he took Dee-Dee out on a date. Mr. Frelund was firm on that rule!

The Carsons lived right next door to our house. Mary Francis called home Five Hundred Dartmouth Drive. She lived at that address with her parents (Ruth and Arden Carson), Paul (her older brother), and Candice (her only sister). Candice was many years older and most of the time away at college in Ann Arbor. She wanted to be a nurse like her mother. The Carsons had lived there for almost two years before we moved in. We were the newcomers to the neighborhood. Mary Francis and I started kindergarten together at Robert Kerr Elementary School.

Daddy and Mamma both worked real hard at giving their four little girls, me and my three sisters, a good start on life. We moved to the newly developed subdivision when I was just five years old. *My baby sister wasn't even born yet!* Daddy built our new house himself while we were living at Grandpa's and Grandma's two-story home in a small sleepy town only four miles away. Our new house was a modest three bedroom, brick, ranch-style. It was perfect for our family, and special to all of us because Daddy had built it. Mamma and Daddy had chosen to relocate in the town where Mamma had graduated from high school. It was pleasing the way our house fit in so nicely with the other new brick, ranch-styles you could see up and down the block. Our neighborhood was on the edge of a railroad town, located in the heart of Michigan.

Daddy was a building contractor. Some folks called him a carpenter, but he could do almost anything and everything related to building a house. He could lay blocks, pour cement, build chimneys, put in electric and plumbing, plaster walls and ceilings, and design a whole house all by himself. It was plain to see that he was more than just a carpenter (which has to do mostly with woodworking, though he was awful good at that part, too). Some people said he had a natural talent for it. People from all over the county were hiring him for work, building and remodeling houses for them, replacing kitchen cabinets, etc. Daddy and Joe, his partner, worked long days through all the seasons of the year. Klco and Cole Building Contractors was a name worth remembering. Daddy had a slogan for the business painted on his truck:

KIco & Cole Builders.
Quality Work: Reasonable Rates.

Families with lots of kids, mostly boys, lived on the surrounding streets. All of us definitely within yelling and spying range of each other. More play pals lived one or two streets over and on the backside of our block. There sure wasn't a shortage of playmates in our neighborhood! Our backyards backed up into each other's. A massive open area for playing existed right in our own backyards. It was a town full of big families with many kids. Everyone, even the moms in the neighborhood, liked it that way. It was easier keeping close track of what was going on with everybody. As soon as someone under the age of twelve was out the door and into the yard, so were half a dozen other kids.

There were kids living in houses up and down the streets, no matter which side of those streets. The five Cameron kids lived, only three blocks down, next to Trumble Park. Marsha, Katie, and Laurie were the three oldest, in that order, and were our schoolmates at Robert Kerr. The two youngest Cameron kids weren't in school yet, just like my two younger sisters. Katie hung out with Mary Francis and me most of the time. Going over to the Cameron's to play was always fun, because all my sisters each had a playmate just about their age and Mamma and Mrs. Cameron were friends.

No other family in town had all the play equipment any kid could hope for right in their own backyard. No wonder most of the school-aged children, on our side of the tracks in town, could be found in the Cameron yard. All playing on the side of the house which bordered the park. Every day spent at Trumble Park, found plenty of kids around. You seldom had to ask twice to find takers who wanted to join in playing an exhausting game of Frozen Tag, Horse, Hide and Seek, or Hop Scotch.

At the park you could pump the swings up as high as you could go without worrying if the swing set would tip over. None of us could resist the Merry-go-Round. Lots of playtime, especially in the summer, was spent hooking our toes beneath the hand bar, leaning out as far as we could, while we spun around and around like a top. Everyone took a turn at pushing... usually without complaint. It wasn't fun listening to the whining of the pushers when it was your turn to fly. It felt great using the warm summer breezes, just created, to dry the salty sweat we had pouring off our dripping bodies.

Looking down on that carousel of flying kids, from my favorite and commonly used spot on the highest tree limb nearest to the merry-go-round, reminded me of the sprockets that spun around inside of Grandpa's gold pocket watch. He would sometimes open the back of his special, antique time piece, for me to take a peek. I watched with amazement, as those little spokes whirled in time. Yep, those sun-bleached heads-of-hair and golden-tanned limbs sticking straight out appeared just like those pointed shiny gold sprockets spinning round and round with no intention of stopping.

One of the most important things about Mrs. Cameron, besides being generous and having lots of kids of her own, was that she always served up treats for all the neighborhood kids to share. Gingersnap windmill cookies were my favorite, or a handful of animal circus cookies might be the choice of the day. A frosty-cold pitcher of orange or red Kool-Aid was also served to help wash them down. With tummies and thirsts satisfied, we would start in singing camp fire songs, *Mickey Mouse Club* favorites, the *Howdy Doody*

Show theme song, or the jingles from the Kool-Aid, Campbell's Soup, Ovaltine, and Kellogg's breakfast cereal ads that we had memorized from the radio and T.V. We would belt out the song *"Happy Trails to You"*, from the *Roy Rogers and Dale Evans Show*. For the sake of entertaining our younger brothers and sisters, we would loudly recite the *Romper Room* chant.

Each day, at four o'clock on the dot, from the *Romper Room* televised broadcast, Miss Martha shared this familiar ditty as she gazed through her sparkly magic mirror. Our magic mirror was an old tennis racket, with broken strings. Mimicking her voice, we proclaimed:

"Romper, Bomper... Stomper Boo,
Tell me, tell me, tell me do,
Did all my friends have fun at school today?"

Every voice under the age of ten screamed out, "YES!" in response to the question.

Then just as if Miss Martha had really heard an answer through the television set, she would again call out from behind her magic mirror... we continued mimicking her with our performance:

"Let's take a look, Boys and Girls. Which of
my friends were **good** at school today?"

All hands would raise in unison, of course! Then on the act would go...

"Oh yes, I see...Suzie and Jimmy.
And there's Annie, Bobby, and
Vicky too," Miss Martha cooed.
"Magic Mirror sees Mary Ann and Billy Joe
who were very good at school today.

And there's Timmy, Tommy,
and Tina watching.
Until tomorrow then... Be good boys and
girls. Remember, eat all of your vegetables."

She'd finish with that rule or another; using a different one each day. One of my favorites was the Golden Rule, "Do unto others as you would have them do unto you." Miss Martha followed that predictable routine picking common names that always fit somebody watching.

We took turns being Miss Martha and leading the charade. All those gathered around, enjoying the fun, used the names of siblings to complete the verses. Younger brothers and sisters present were visibly delighted to have their names used in a game that they knew so well. We sang our hearts out as we enjoyed our refreshment from all the hard playing we had just finished. We harmonized, sang in rounds, and laughed 'til our stomachs hurt.

We spent a great deal of time together most every day. Baseball and war were our favorite choices for games. Mamma got irritated at having to buy Band-Aids for the army all the time. I tried to explain that Clara Barton would never have made it if it weren't for having a full supply of bandages when she needed them. With Mary Francis and me being the army nurses there was no other choice in the matter. Mamma could sure see my point and agreed there was nothing left to be done, except to keep buying Band-Aids, which she did.

We shared very large play areas where our backyards came together. The subdivision was not finished, so empty lots dotted the scene on almost every block. We always played ball in the vacant lot across the street from Mary Francis' house and right next door to the Frelunds. Almost every day there was a baseball or softball game played there, because the boys insisted on that! Our war zone was in the empty lot right next door to our house on the opposite side from Mary Francis's house. We sure were sad when Mrs. Waters built her house there, two years after we moved into the neighborhood.

There were discarded building supplies left laying around on lots from some of the new houses that had been recently built. Those made great bunkers and foxholes to hide behind when we sided up and took on an enemy. We got shovels and dug holes. We dragged the wood around and built walls and fortresses to our hearts' delight. Sometimes we were the Americans fighting the German Gestapo. Other times we were the Union soldiers fighting the Confederates. Other times it was cowboys against indians, indians against cowboys, or cowboys against bandits. Even George Washington crossing the Delaware took place right in our own neighborhood. The Patriots usually had their day against the English troops of King George, and of course, in the end, the Americans were always on the winning side.

You would have thought the bullets were really flying to hear all the yelling and commanding that was going on. The boys worked hard at perfecting the art of faking a very realistic combat wound, as they fell to the ground in the throes of death. Two soldiers from the same side would run out from behind their plywood fortress, stoop low to the ground, grab their wounded buddy by both arms and drag their comrade back to safety. Not even two minutes later, you'd see that same fallen soldier stick his head up from behind the battered wall, very much alive, and he'd start firing at the enemy again. That would go on for hours. No wonder it took so many boxes of Band-Aids to keep

TERESA LEE

that troop doctored up. No Red Cross medics were worth their weight if they didn't take good care of their soldiers, and slap on the bandages, and revive them from a mortal wound. We loved our pretend world where the reality of war had no place; where no one ever really died.

We used the very large lot next to Nelson's to ride our horses. As sheriffs and deputies we planned surprise attacks on pesky bandits, from the tall picky grass. We laid in wait for bad guys to ride in or out of "Dodge City." Those who wanted to play, took turns and drew sticks to choose up sides. The unlucky kids, who drew the two or three shortest toothpicks for the day, had to be the bandits. The in-between sized toothpicks had to be the deputies of "Sheriff Matt Dillon of Dodge City"; all anxiously waiting and ready to follow his every command. The longest toothpick (the cherished prize) got to be Matt Dillon. He was the best sheriff in the West! He starred in *Gunsmoke,* one of the favorite T.V. Western shows most kids watched on a regular basis. Our dads were usually the first ones on the couch at the start of the show. Actually, we thought it great fun to be the bad guys, since our mothers would have none of that behavior in real life.

In the summer when school was out, it was playtime from morning to dusk and if we were lucky, dark. Most summer nights when the windows were open to grab the breezes and cool the house, you could hear the sound of water running as it filled the bathtubs up and down the block. Those dirty bathtub rings told the story of just how much play had gone on that day. The rip of Band-Aids coming off, followed by muffled yells were part of the evening summer sounds up and down every street for blocks around.

Chapter Three

Sailing

The map Mary Francis and Leggins used in finding the way to becoming best friends included some difficult days. A few that ended with black eyes, scratches, snow washed faces and fat lips. We survived yelling at each other, pulling hair, throwing crayons and sometimes not speaking for days. Friendship isn't always easy!

About the first thing you couldn't help noticing when coming in our back door was that shining expanse of black tiled, kitchen floor that Mamma took a good deal of pride in polishing. She worked real hard at keeping it so shiny you could see yourself in it, just like looking at your reflection in a quiet pond. Friday was the day, every single week, that she scrubbed it shiny clean on her hands and knees, whether it needed it or not. My sisters and I never missed the chance to take advantage of the full effect that a half bottle of Johnson and Johnson Liquid Floor Wax had on that surface. In less than an hour, that floor dried to a high gloss brilliance that screamed, "Smooth as glass! All sliders, WELCOME!" Dried to perfection, that wax made the floor slippery like an eel! In the summer, Mamma would even set motion fans in each of the two doorways and let them run until the floor had no sticky spot any-where. My sisters and I lived for the opportunity to answer the sliding invitation that floor offered up.

When Mamma would take a quick trip to the grocery store and Daddy was busy working on something outside or in the basement, my sisters and I used to stand at the farthest end of the living room carpet and run as fast as we could straight ahead to the edge of the doorway leading into the kitchen. We squealed with delight sliding on socked feet the full length of that beautiful shining slippery black ocean. If we got a good start we could surf clear to the line of salmon colored cupboards at the other end. It was always a game to see who would sail the fastest and farthest. We held our own contests and never forgot who had won the last time we sailed!

Mamma usually was never the wiser for it, except when my sisters slipped right before they got to the wall of cupboards and slid with a full body slam right into those doors. We were young and not very big in size, so it never really amounted to much damage or pain. Exceptions of course: When Jackie, my sister who was fifteen months younger than me, got her black eye from hitting it on the cupboard door handle. Ouch, that hurt! Another time Christie, my sister who was three years younger than me, broke her toenail and sprained her foot from hitting the face board under the cupboard door at full force. That was damage we couldn't explain away. Jackie and I got in big trouble for that one, with Mamma's words stinging, "You know better. You are older. She's too little to know she shouldn't do that." Following those two episodes and for weeks after, whenever Mamma left the house she would always call from the garage, "Girls, remember, **No Sailing**!"

Mamma believed that she had the prettiest kitchen on our street. It bragged a long, L-shaped set of peachy pink painted cupboards at one end. They edged the dark glittering floor and ran from the end of the sink around to the Double Dutch door, which was kept latched only on the bottom. It looked like half a door with a ledge for leaning on and looking into the kitchen. When the Dutch door opened, you stepped down two steps to a landing that most people called "the breezeway". Directly left was a long flight of stairs that went straight down to our large cement block basement. To the right of the landing, and two steps down, were the double doors that led out to our single car garage. A storm door with double paned glass, necessary for keeping out the winter cold, always stood open during the summer months. The screened door led directly outside to the garage and was used from spring through autumn. It allowed in those welcomed summertime breezes, and stood guard keeping out most all of the pesky warm weather insects.

Mosquitoes were the worst! Our attached garage had a screened-in porch on its backside that we used every day and on hot sticky nights of the summer. Many Michigan houses had screened-in porches because of those nasty, blood-sucking bugs. Summertime picnics were more tolerable due to those wonderful porches offering up protection from flying, biting, or crawling pests. Mamma hated flies in the house and couldn't abide a spider of any sort! The screens were always in place at our house throughout the warmest of the summer months.

One early day in our friendship found me and Mary Francis standing face to face across our backyard property lines. We were shaking our fists ferociously and pointing grubby little fingers each other's way: Daring the other to step over the line. Our raised voices declared boldly what awful fate was sure to happen if a toe so much as crossed that imaginary line. Each of us hoping secretly that the dare wasn't taken.

"Don't you dare step on my poppity!" Mary Francis screeched from her side of the yard. At the age of five, sometimes the words didn't come out right.

"I come in your yard if I want to, and you can't do anything! I'm telling my mamma what a mean girl you are!" My angry words spilled out.

"I'm never gonna let you touch my dog again! You aren't my friend!" Mary Francis threatened.

"You're not my friend neither! You are a bad girl! Besides, you look funny with no front teeth!" came my nasty reply.

Things were going south fast, as Mary Francis grabbed my blouse and threw me to the ground. I started screaming to the top of my lungs. I grabbed Mary Francis by the leg and pulled her down. We were kicking each other and crying. Suddenly, each of our mothers grabbed their own child by an arm and yanked us both to our feet. This skirmish ended with a stern motherly intervention.

"Young Lady, you will stop this fighting immediately!" came my mother's stern command. "**Both** of you, stop this instant!" were her rushing words, as my little sisters stood staring wide-eyed from behind her skirts.

Mary Francis and I stood eye-to-eye faces stained with grass, dirt, and tears. The fight in each of us suddenly drained away. *I don't care if I get a spanking! I am not saying, sorry!*

"Girls, you **will** apologize to each other **right now** and **mean** it! What kind of behavior is this for two

TERESA LEE

friends?" Mrs. Carson accused. "I'm ashamed of your behavior, Mary Francis!" Her mother finished with a scowl. Her eyebrows knitted tight together.

We were both forced to say "Sorry." While our mothers held us firmly by the shoulder. Each of us held tears in our eyes, a body as straight as a board and a voice that mumbled the attempt at showing our remorse. After the apologies were said we were promptly grounded from seeing each other for the remainder of the week and sent to our rooms. The day it all happened we didn't even care. *Who wants a bad girl like that for a friend? NOT ME! I've got my sisters! And I don't care about her dog either!* Which was of course, not true. I sure believed that I was never ever going to speak to that Mary Francis Carson again!

That sentiment changed mighty fast! After the first few days of our sentence, sheer misery set in. At the first opportunity, we were circling to the backside of the block, out of the sight of our dear mothers, grabbing hands and running off to play, while the smiles on our faces stretched from ear to ear. We always found our way back to each other. Days later, after all was made up, we never seemed to recall just why we got so mad in the first place.

Yes, that was Mary Francis and me. In many ways we were as different as night and day, but we never stayed mad at each other for long. We were in and out of each other's houses like a summer breeze drifting about through open screens, sailing to our very own friends-for-life destination. At our young age, we didn't even recognize what we had when we had it. All we really knew was that we had the best times whenever we were together. Over time, we discovered a best friend treasure in each other.

Chapter Four

Chilled Mugs to Go!

Best friends are good for each other. They are better together than apart, like frosting on a cupcake, socks that match, or candy and Halloween. You can have one without the other, but it's not as good. You fit together like a hand and glove. Life seems to get better after you find your best friend treasure. You are always looking forward to tomorrow and the adventures it will bring. When it comes to genuine friendship, you try to put your best foot forward. You want your best friend to think that you are one of the most special people they know.

Jackie, my next younger sister, Mary Francis and I loved to play one of our favorite games right there in that wonderful breezeway. We pretended that the Dutch door leading into the kitchen was an ordering window at an A & W Drive-In Root-Beer Stand. On rainy days when we had to keep the garage door down or on hot summer days when we could put it up, we took turns "waitressing or working in the kitchen". One of us would stand inside the kitchen on one side of the swinging door, 'cooking' the orders and filling them. Meanwhile, the other two were outside the door, going back and forth, up and down the two short flights of stairs, between the garage and kitchen. We were busy as bees taking the orders and serving them to the lines of imaginary cars parked two steps down. Sometimes the neighborhood kids would ride their bikes in and line them up so they could be the customers we aimed to please. We'd stand looking over the double Dutch door, calling out orders to each other and using waitress lingo like,

"Hold the mayo on that B.L.T."

Or "Make that a double order of onion rings, easy on the salt!"

Then maybe, "Two large suds, chilled mugs to go!"

Kool-Aid made by the pitcher (only one flavor) served as our ice-cold A&W Root Beer beverage. The chilled mug of imaginary root beer was passed off in a small bathroom Dixie Cup filled half way up with that yummy Kool-Aid nectar. We had to be very careful not to spill and also make the "Root Beer" last as long as possible, since that was the cheapest we could manage. No one ever complained though, because on a hot and humid summer day in Michigan anything wet tasted good. It was swell! After all, Mamma never allowed pop of any kind in our house. We didn't want to push our luck; for the pantry was sure to be off limits if we presumed to take advantage of our good situation. Running an A&W Root-Beer Stand was a little worrisome but a lot of fun!

We had to depend entirely on Mamma's kind generosity to provide the pantry items we used to produce our very own A&W menu. We carefully cut out and copied onto the sides of old used brown-paper sacks the tasty entrees being served that day. Of course, we gave them proper names that would raise a customer's curiosity about what it might be that they were ordering. Some of our more popular fares were given catchy titles on the menu. Roller Skate Surprise (a Ritz cracker with the "chef's" creativity given expression), Flies on a Brick (chocolate chips stuck in peanut butter on top of a zwieback cracker), Canoeing in Winter (a small celery stalk filled with cream cheese and dotted with two raisins), The Drowning Midge (a raisin floating in a glass of root beer flavored Kool-Aid) were just a few of the mouth-watering selections. It was easy to see why our customers were always lining up for more!

Running an "A&W Root Beer Stand" was hard, sweaty work. The appointed cook, "working the kitchen" slapped on whatever condiment topping Mamma felt like sharing that day (peanut butter, jelly, jam, cream cheese or Cheez Whiz). No more than two selections per customer, per play session, on crackers (Zwieback, Nabisco Saltines, or Ritz) plopped down on a paper plate. Sometimes to add a special flare, we would add seasonal fruit, like cut up apples. Blueberries were another favorite. The only acceptable vegetables were salted tomatoes or cucumbers right out of the garden. Yum! Maybe carrot sticks, if Mamma had an overabundance in the salad crisper. That was about all the vegetables you could slip by anyone under the age of twelve without an argument! The onion rings were round pretzels, compliments of the stash that Mary Francis always kept under her bed! The "chef" would pass the ordered entrée to the waiting "waitress" in less than three minutes. I always wondered if all A&W customers were as impatient as ours seemed to be. We had to work fast. After all, we couldn't have our customers leaving empty-handed or waiting long to get a nice cold drink! No one would ever come back! Whew!

Mary Francis, Jackie, and I knew without a doubt that A&W waitressing jobs were some of the hardest to come by for a girl. So, all the practice we could get sure wouldn't hurt. Just knowing how to roller skate well enough took real talent. Skating up to the window of a waiting car to take an order was hard enough with only a pencil and pad in your hand. However, delivering a tray loaded with food and liquid beverages was another challenge altogether!

An A&W waitressing job demanded not spilling root beer or any other edible item from the order of a customer waiting to be served. *How exactly is that done? And while roller skating no less? This would take some training!* Usually the "line of cars" in our garage was noisy and very demanding. Not one of our customers cut us a minute of slack and we knew we had best be getting our jobs done or we'd be hearing all about it. A skinned knee or rude comment usually ended the fun, but we never tired of the routine.

Another thing we knew for certain... a girl couldn't have just any common kind of name to get a job at an A&W Root-Beer Stand. You had to be lucky enough to be born with a perky name like Trixie or Patsy. Our proof was living right across the street. Mike Frelund's older sister, Dee-Dee, was a drive-in A&W girl. Who has a name like hers? All the A&W Root-Beer girls had names like that. They were catchy like Dotty, Dinie, Tina, Laura Lee or Billie Joe was good, too. Mostly those names ending in that long stretched out e-e-e... got those jobs right off. We also were fairly certain that no one ever got an A&W job whose bad luck it was to have a name like Hortense, Ruby, or Gertrude. The same went for Mabel or Blanche, like my grandma, who had to settle for being a teacher.

Yep, those were glamorous jobs all right! What exactly was it that caused the boys to get all starry eyed over those A&W girls anyway? You could tell the girls loved their jobs, being able to get away with wearing those short skirts and roller skates while they served up cold root beer and the best hamburgers around. Pretty smiles and long swinging ponytails, seemed to be necessities for those jobs, as the steady rhythm of the jukebox music filled the air. We all guessed that being an A&W Girl was about the best job any girl could hope for. We planned on doing that for sure, since we all had names that ended just right. Mary, Terry, Jackie, Christie, Cathy. Yes Sir, we had a good chance if we could only learn how to skate without falling down.

Chapter Five

Moderate Chop

Discovering a best friend is like finding a treasure. Sometimes a best friend can be very hard to find. Other times people bump into their best friend by accident. Situations can unfold when two people just get shoved together because of something that happens, and "Voila!"(That's French for "there it is!") Your life becomes richer in an instant. As treasures go, sometimes you spend a lot of time trying to figure out if it's the real thing. The treasure might be tarnished and not have that expected sparkly look. You may have to polish it up, after you've scraped away all the crusty dirt and debris. Let's just say that at first sight "diamonds in the rough" may be hard to recognize as real treasures.

Mary Francis and I got along about as well as anybody ever had. Anyway that's what Mary Francis thought and I can promise you she wasn't the easiest person a body ever had to get along with! If Mary Francis said it was so, I guessed it was!

You had to look at things real close to get a bit of understanding as to why Mary Francis carried on so sometimes. She was into what grownups call 'throwing tantrums' when things didn't go her way. Things didn't go her way a lot, so you can imagine what life could be like living around Mary Francis. She'd start kicking and screaming, sometimes right out in the yard or in a store when she wanted something and wasn't getting it. If she really wanted to get everybody all stirred up, she'd commence on holding her breath 'til she turned blue and fainted dead away. I knew she'd be all right. I'd seen her come out of it enough times before. Though, it sure did get the grown-ups jumping around like grasshoppers.

Folks nearby would start wringing their hands, while Mary Francis was making her views known concerning a particular situation. People passing by would roll their eyes and heave out air from their chests like that was going to make Mary Francis stop. She never paid them any mind that I could see. It didn't take long and her Mamma would drag her (still kicking and screaming) into the house, out to the car or better yet, give her what she wanted in the first place. If her mom didn't give it to her, somebody else nearby usually did; just to shut her up.

Mary Francis prided herself regularly on using tantrums to get her way. On several occasions and with a purposeful smile, when her parents weren't looking, she let me know that had been her plan. I never counted on getting away with a plan like that. My Daddy had informed me that if I ever had figured on trying out a tantrum, I'd get my backside tanned good and proper and have difficulty sitting for a spell. I guessed it wasn't for me. My sisters and I knew for

TERESA LEE

certain sure, with no exceptions, Daddy meant what he said. We didn't need to test the waters on that one!

Mary Francis' parents owned and operated the drugstore in town. Her mamma and daddy worked every day... all day... at 'The Store.' Most all the mothers in the neighborhood were housewives and were home every day, but not Mary Francis' mother. Mary's mother had quit her nursing career years earlier to help in the drugstore every day. Mrs. Carson wasn't home, as much as most of the other moms were, but she could be if the need arose. Which it sometimes did, when it came to Mary Francis.

Mary Francis had one older sister, Candice Marie and an older brother, Paul. Candice Marie was 15 years older than Mary so she wasn't around much. She was living and studying at a nursing school. She was set on being a nurse like her Mom, who didn't do nursing anymore but knew how. When Candice Marie did come home which wasn't often, she didn't talk to Mary Francis much. Mary thought Candice was "the best thing since sliced bread", as grandma used to say, when she really like something special. Candice was usually too busy studying and being all dreamy-eyed over her boy-friend, James. So on most weekends she was too busy to spend any time with Mary. Mr. James Drake was studying at being a doctor, which Mary Francis said her mamma and daddy thought was real respectable. Candice Marie told Mary Francis in one of her 'un-busy' moments that she fully intended on marrying Mr. James Drake at the earliest possible opportunity. Mary Francis ran right over to give me the word. She made me promise not to tell a soul or she'd set about throw-ing the biggest tantrum I'd ever seen, if she found out I had snitched. Of course, I didn't.

Mary Francis didn't always get along well with her older and only brother, which wasn't that unusual as siblings go. She and Paul were often fussing at each other and disagreeing over just about everything there was to disagree about. They would usually keep it up until their parents sent them to their rooms, or one locked the other out of the house. They were always doing that! Some days, they would fight from morning until night. They never seemed to tire of the aggravation they passed out so generously to each other. When Mary couldn't stand it one more minute, she would usually come over to our house to play and wait until her parents came home from the store for dinner. Paul was then left to his own entertainment for the rest of the day, which then no longer included tormenting his youngest sister.

Mary Francis and Paul made it a regular everyday game to take a favorite belonging of the other and hide it. They would act all innocent, like they didn't have the slightest idea where that favorite belonging could be. The one whose favorite item would be missing would start tearing the house apart looking for it. On one particular day, Paul had hidden something belonging to his sister. Mary Francis started throwing everything out of Paul's drawers and closets. She was racing all around the house looking in all the nooks and crannies where her favorite things had been hidden before.

"Paul Carson, you tell me where my piggy bank is right this minute, or I'm telling mother that you stole my allowance!" Mary Francis yelled.

"Who said I took your stupid piggy bank? Besides, why would I want it with only two quarters in it?" John snapped back.

"How would you know that, unless you had swiped it in the first place?!" came Mary's accusation. She raced to his room to snag something of value that he would hate her having. Spying his Boy Scout sash, with all his hard earned badges attached and hanging from the knob on the closet door, Mary Francis grabbed it. She promptly dashed out the door leading to the back hall and her room; slamming the door behind her. Paul started pounding on her bedroom door, in a rage to get his Boy Scout sash back. Too late, she had already shoved her bed against it to keep him out.

The search had come to a standstill. The piggy bank wasn't being found, and Mary Francis now had his cherished badge sash. Of course, Paul had done the hiding of the piggy bank. However, now he couldn't stand one more minute of the thought: Mary Francis had one of his most prized possessions in her clutches.

She wasn't helping the situation as she sang cheerily from behind the door, "I've got your badges! Too, bad for you-u-u!"

So came Paul's one little clue, uttered through the closed and barricaded door, hoping she'd come out. "Find your piggy at a trough, where you'll never see a moth!" he chirped in a sing-song voice.

That action gave him away as being the culprit. Standing in the hall, we both heard the bed slide away from the closed door. Only seconds passed and Mary's bedroom door flew open. No sash in hand, she tore to the spot figured out from his clue. Paul shot into her room to find his sash. Mary Francis raced into her parents' bedroom. I knew from experience that if that piggy bank was not found in her mother's cedar chest, somewhere among all those woolen sweaters, and the sash wasn't located immediately, due to his frantic search of her bedroom, the fighting was about to commence! That was my cue. I high-tailed it out of there before the throwing of punches, biting, and kicking got underway.

Most days when Mary Francis's mom and dad worked at the store, Paul was home alone with his youngest sister. They would set about doing their required chores around the house. Paul could be mean to Mary Francis. He'd set about pinching her and hitting her with the wet end of a dish towel trying to get her to do his share of the work for that day. Sometimes he would snap that towel hard on her bare leg, when she wore shorts or shorty pajamas, until it left a red spot. On days I was over at their house, Mary and I would each get a towel and start snapping him right back! Two against one usually sent him flying to his room, which was followed by a slam of the door and a click of the lock. If Mary Francis started on crying and screaming, Paul would tell her that if she told anybody he'd get her good next time and we both believed him. A couple of times she told her parents anyway. Once after she told on him, Paul got a nasty spanking in the garage, with the belt, when her dad got home from work. Mary Francis didn't tattle to anyone else after that, excepting just to me.

One day when I was at the Carson's helping Mary clean the bathrooms, Paul started in on both of us, squirting us over and over with his new squirt gun. He had filled it with water and red food coloring so it looked like blood when he hit us. He was messing up what we had just cleaned, and staining our clothes whenever his shot hit its target, which was us!

"Stop it now or I'll be sharing your mean ways with my daddy when he gets home for lunch!" I snapped. "You can just be explaining to Mamma why this white blouse I'm wearing, which she just laundered and spent precious time ironing, is all stained with red!" I finished with a glare.

Mary Francis looked at me with surprise as I seldom spoke my mind about things. *But I did today!* Paul immediately stopped and ran outside slamming the back storm door as hard as he could, probably hoping the glass would break so he could blame it on Mary

Francis and me. The glass rattled, and shook the frame, but miraculously stayed intact. Both Mary Francis and I smiled at each other with wide eyes, totally shocked, but glad to have that pest out of our hair for a while. I figured that Paul remembered real well what had happened when I had told on him to my Daddy once before.

On that occasion, upon hearing my breathless and tearful story, Daddy had risen quickly from the table. With purpose, he placed his fork and napkin on the table, left his lunch on his plate uneaten, put his boots back on at the garage steps, and marched over to the Carson's house. He proceeded to share several sharp words of warning into Paul's ear, which was being held tightly by my father's fingers at the time! Mary and I had heard it all as we stood in the side yard beneath Mary's open bedroom window. Later that same day, when Mr. and Mrs. Carson got home from work, my dad met them in their driveway and they all stood talking quietly for some time. Paul was grounded for a week after that episode. He knew my daddy meant business and wasn't putting up with all his nonsense. It was a threat that always miraculously halted Paul's torment of teasing and nasty reprisals.

Mr. and Mrs. Carson worked real hard on keeping their store's business going strong. They seemed tired a lot of the time. Neither one talked much. Mostly when they were off work they sat at the kitchen table, read the newspaper, smoked cigarettes (like many folks did) and drank a lot of hot, black coffee. Mary and Paul were better behaved and more quiet when their parents were at home, at least most of the time.

Mary Francis usually wanted to do all her house chores real spic and span like, so she'd get her weekly allowance of $1.00 every Saturday. She would make deals with me so that I would help her get the work done, then together we'd spend that allowance. Some warm summer days, the Good Humor Ice Cream Man would wind his way into our neighborhood. While driving his truck with the musical jingle filling the air, the expected begging would begin for just enough coins to buy a refreshing ice cream treat. Mary Francis would run for her stash of allowance, usually hidden somewhere safe in her room. She never hid it in the same place twice, just in case Paul was of a mind to snoop. Back she'd come as quick as a wink! We'd split it and hand it over with smiling faces to the Good Humor man in return for a Fudgy Nut Ice Cream bar, or a chocolate and vanilla, nut-covered, ice cream drumstick.

Mary was very honest about keeping the bargain. Most Saturdays we'd take our hard earned money and without blinking an eye, eagerly lay down fifteen cents each for a yummy, melt in your mouth, cream-filled triangle. Every bite found that creamy sweet filling squishing out both sides of your mouth. *Better than candy!* Those soft warm rolls made you nearly faint with the goodness of their taste. They were baked fresh, three times a week, at the bakery downtown. We'd sit on the wooden bench outside her Daddy's store, that is if Boxcar Joe wasn't occupying his usual spot there, and savor every bite of those warm, taste-bud busters. Nothing ever could be better! So, since I always wanted to be in on the spending of that hard earned dollar every Saturday, and not miss out on my creamy triangle fix, I spent a good amount of time helping out with the Carson's chores.

Sometimes on hot sticky summer nights when everybody had their windows open, it was easier to hear family disagreements. Most families had them from time to time. The whole neighborhood was only trying to get any little breath of a breeze, through the screens. There wouldn't be a leaf stirring. Everything seemed hot and heavy. (You couldn't help but hear a fuss going on in the neighborhood.) Sometimes it was Mary Francis or Paul screaming at each other. Other times it was Mary or Paul screaming at their mother. Once in a while it would be Mr. and Mrs. Carson that were disagreeing. Out of the corner of my eye, as my sisters all stared at their plates, when we were eating dinner at the kitchen table, or sometimes watching T.V. in the evening, I would see Mamma look over at Daddy. She didn't think I saw that sad worried look that crossed over one to the other, but I did. I worried too, and my tummy always felt like it was in knots when that fighting would begin. I seldom heard fighting like that, not in my house or in most other homes I visited with my parents and grandparents. It was a sure thing that life at the Carson's could be stormy.

Grandpa used to say, "Sometimes life is like a ship sailing on an ocean with moderate chop." He often used the word 'chop' to talk about rough waters on a lake. When we were in the boat at the lake in the summer he would complain, "If this chop would settle down a bit, we might be lucky and get in some good fishin' before dark."

Daddy explained, "Grandpa meant, life can be rough! Everybody, at one time or another, experiences it. You've got to keep the bow of your boat...or your life... going in the right direction. Slow down your speed... take more time when things get rough. You have to learn to deal with the conditions you've been given," Daddy finished my grandfather's meaning.

I thought it must be like when Grandpa and Daddy would keep bailing out our rowboat so that it didn't take on too much water and sink. In life, managing the everyday stuff (in the best way you know how) is the hard part. That's what keeps things steady.

"Sometimes when things in life seem hard," Grandpa would say, "Staying afloat is the thing. Keep your oars in the water. It helps with balance and keeps the boat movin' forward. Even if it takes time gettin' where you need to be, stay focused on the shore and where you want to go. With hard work and patience, you'll get there."

I guessed that the Carson family was experiencing their sail through life in an ocean with moderate chop. Smooth days meant the waves or chop was light and easier to manage; not much drama when it came to Mary Francis and how she was managing. On days when things were far from calm, the waves or chop was forceful and harder to manage; disagreements and tantrums followed by sleepless nights. Let's just say that some days were certainly rougher than others. Mary Francis was living proof of the effect a life lived with moderate chop could produce. Those restless nights from tension and stress took their toll on her. It was always the same after a bad night.

Next morning, Mary Francis would appear at our door. Her eyes all red and puffy from crying, hair sticking straight up all over her head in every direction. She hadn't even taken the time to comb it after another night of tossing and turning. She would sneak out of the house, as quick as her daddy had left for the store. She knew her mamma would stay in bed most of the day after a bad night, because she always did. I guessed it was real hard running a big store like theirs. With so many worries, it was bound to make you mad and irritable sometimes.

Even at that early hour of the morning, my mamma would put her arms around Mary Francis and bring her into the kitchen. She'd brush her hair real nice and wash Mary's face before she'd let her eat. Then Mamma would set Mary Francis down at our kitchen table and give her the biggest fresh-baked cookie she could find in the cookie jar, along with a cold glass of milk. Sometimes, that peeved me. My sisters and I weren't allowed cookies until after our afternoon naps and only if we had eaten our lunch up good and proper. We never got cookies in the morning!

After a few of these episodes, I figured it was fair enough, on account of Mary Francis' mother not having time to bake cookies and Mary Francis feeling so bad. I wondered if that was why Mary Francis always appeared on our doorstep every morning after one of those nights. Had she wanted the cookies and milk to make her feel better, or Mamma's arms around her warm and loving? No wonder Mary Francis spent most of her summer days and after school hours at our house. I couldn't really hold it against her because after all, she was my best friend. I hated it when she was sad, and we all loved her like she was a part of our family. Grandma used to say, "In this family there is love enough for everyone!" *That was the truth, especially when it came to Mary Francis.*

Chapter Six

The Peanut Caper

With your best friend, that beautiful side eventually shines out for you to appreciate and you're hooked. Your favorite pal becomes the golden one that you want to spend your time with, share secrets with, laugh and play games with, even when you are mad or feeling sad. Sometimes best friends find each other because they like the same things or think the same way. Best friends laugh together easily, and find similar circumstances funny. Others are tight because they are opposites. One friend fills gaps for the other friend. Together you're better.

My first clear understanding that Mary Francis was hopping mad about things at home was when she stuffed that warm salted peanut clear up her nose and let it stay there for two weeks. That action of course created the fiercest nosebleeds, and all just to make her Mamma and Daddy pay her some attention. Many months later, just between the two of us, we named it the "Peanut Caper."

At first no one could figure out why Mary Francis' nose was suddenly taken to such extreme bleeding. Her Mamma had to stay home from work and Mary Francis had to stay home from school on account of never knowing when it would start in spewing blood again. It was bad enough when it started bleeding, but the biggest worry was how to get it to stop once it had started! Her nose would start seeping red around her nostrils and begin the downward drip off from her chin. It took forever to get the bleeding stopped, and a whole pile of white washcloths turned bright red from the trying. We would pinch the bridge of her nose, tilt her head back, put an ice pack on the bridge of her nose, stuff her nose with tissues or cotton balls, or have Mary Francis lay down on the floor with her head back. Every now and then, that didn't work and she would cough up the blood. There were times when she had to endure all of the remedies in the same session. Nose bleeds were becoming something we dreaded.

Once when the bleeding would not quit, her mother wrapped a long elastic bandage around and around her face across the bridge of her nose, with a thick gauze pad underneath that covered her nostrils. Mrs. Carson pulled the bandage tight so that Mary Francis could only breathe through her mouth. After about a half hour, the bleeding slowed. The bandage was soaked with blood, but eventually that method worked. After a few days of staying home due to continuous nose bleeds, Mary's mom finally got fed up with the whole mess and toted her off to the doctor.

You can well imagine everyone's surprise when the doctor announced it was all on account of an old peanut he'd found wedged in good and tight, clear up inside the nose of Miss Mary Francis Carson. Doc

TERESA LEE

Mason took on something awful when he'd discovered the cause. He started in questioning Mary Francis right off, wondering how a peanut that size got wedged in there in the first place. Mary Francis, not wanting to take the blame for the muddled up mess she'd got herself into, said it was a real simple thing that happened, and started in explaining. Miss Mary Francis put all the blame on that tempting peanut case at her dad's drugstore.

According to Mary, this is how the whole thing rolled out. Ardith Mayes, one of the drugstore employees, had been filling the store display case of mixed nuts with fresh ones and Mary Francis stood by just watching her do it. Anyone walking in the front door couldn't help but notice that warm, salty, roasted peanut aroma, or the shining light bulb that kept those nuts warmed just right. The smell of those fresh nuts was so-o-o good that Mary Francis just couldn't help herself from bending over at the waist and sticking her whole head inside that peanut case.

While Mrs. Mayes was at the back of the store attending to a customer, Mary Francis took a long and powerful sniff of that glorious smell. She figured she must have got a trifle too close and one of those ole peanuts sitting right on top of that mound of golden nuts flew straight up her nose from all that suckin' in and sniffin'. It must have gone up there so far that she didn't even feel it, so didn't know it was even up there…. And that's how it all got started or so she said.

Later, Mary Francis told me she thought that the doctor and her mother were set on believing that story right off, since they looked directly at each other and neither could think of one question to ask about the whole happening.

Mary said, "Yep, they both just sat there staring at each other with their lips pressed tight together. Never could come up with even one more question for me."

Doc Mason wrote out a prescription for medicine to clear up the infection in Mary Francis' nose on account of that nasty peanut setting in there real quiet for two weeks. Furthermore, he was dead certain that was the cause of all the nosebleeds and informed Mary Francis that she best stay clear of that nut case in the future. Mary Francis later shared a mischievous smile with me when she told how she had responded quickly to the doctor's last remark saying, "You don't have to worry a minute about that, because I don't want any part of being around another nut case!" So with a sudden jerk of her arm, off Mary Francis went with her mother, who seemed in a hurry to get out of that doctor's office and back to work.

I talked to Mary Francis at length about the "Peanut Caper." After quite a spell of figurin' it out, we agreed it wasn't the best way to go about getting attention. We thought maybe all those nose bleeds were a might tiresome and perhaps tantrum throwing was a better way. Besides all this, Mary had decided after leaving the doctor's office that she wouldn't be doing anything in the future which caused any doctor to shove a pair of steel tweezers so far up her nose that it made her right eyeball jiggle.

Daddy always had things to say about what went on with Mary Francis, especially when it had to do with doctors having to retrieve foreign objects from her nose, even if it did happen to be a little old peanut. So, when she came over a day or two after being looked over by Doc Mason, my daddy had his say over the "Peanut Caper."

Mary Francis and I had just come back from riding our bikes three times around the block. We came

TERESA LEE

gliding into the cool of the garage for a rest. Daddy had just gotten home from work and was sitting on the back step by the landing taking off his boots; his usual daily routine.

Without looking up, as he unlaced his last boot, he began, "Mary Francis, get over here and set a spell. What's this I hear about you havin' trouble with an old peanut bein' up your nose?" Mary Francis got off her bike instantly and went over to sit on his knee for a minute, which she always loved to do.

Daddy continued, "So, let's have a good close look at this nose problem," he said as he tipped her head back to stare up the nostril in question. After a quiet moment, he tipped her chin down, looking directly into those dark set eyes that were Mary Francis'. Using a firm voice Daddy stated plainly, "I don't want to hear of anything like that ever happening again. It's not fitting that any child should be stuffing something as hurtful as an old peanut up their own nose causing it such grief! Furthermore Mary Francis, you are a very special young'un, same as my own girls, and I am not much taken with anything bad happening to them either. It would surely rest my mind some to know that you will never be trying something like that again. Everyone in the Cole family is always going to love Miss Mary Francis no matter what!" Daddy finished with a gentle tap to her nose.

Big brimfuls of slow rolling, salty tears came streaming down the cheeks of Mary Francis while daddy commenced on speaking his piece. I guessed it was on account that she'd been found out and all. Mary Francis hung her head down real low and all those tears started dripping off her chin onto Daddy's tee shirt leaving wet spots wherever they fell, then quick as anything she threw her arms tight around Daddy's neck. They sat like that, real quiet, for a minute or two then he swung her up onto his shoulders as her tears began turning into smiles. I watched as Daddy ran with Mary Francis through the screened in porch out into the backyard in his stocking feet with no thought about the grass stains he'd surely get on the bottoms or the scolding from mamma he'd be taking for doing it. As Daddy ran, circling the backyard, with Mary Francis laughing and screaming like it was her last day for living and Daddy tickling her knees and smiling real big, I knew that Mary Francis wouldn't feel the need to stick peanuts up her nose anymore. I just couldn't figure out how Daddy had known it all along, but I sure was thankful that he did. My dad was one of the people that I loved more than anyone else in the entire world, and right at that moment I was certain Mary Francis did, too.

Chapter Seven

Perks

Friends listen to each other; most of the time that is. At least, you try very hard. The same person doesn't always get to do all the talking or go first every time. With Mary Francis and me, that was a challenge, but we worked it out between us. Friends take turns willingly and learn to share with a happy heart. Which was yet another challenge we managed to overcome eventually.

One of you might not be good at drawing, but the other is, so you can get a project done better, by doing it together. True again, only if you don't end up throwing the pencils and crayons at each other, as occasionally happened with me and Mary Francis. I drew the backgrounds. Mary drew the people. I wasn't good at drawing people or animals, but she was. Mary Francis could draw dogs like a pro. Especially collies, because she had one. Your friend might be able to talk easily to others and you are shy. Mary Francis was seldom shy. I was happy about that, because I was timid and she usually did most of the talking. The important thing was that Mary Francis and I made a great team. That's what true friends do.

It didn't appear to me, all things considered, that Mary Francis had it so bad, though mamma hinted that her situation wasn't the best. She got a one dollar allowance every Saturday, which my sisters and I never got. We did more helping around the house in one day, than Mary Francis did in a whole week! Daddy said working in a family and for your family built character and nobody should be getting paid for their character getting built up, which was a benefit to their own self anyway.

Besides the allowance grudge, Mary Francis had the most beautiful golden colored collie dog any kid could ever hope to have. Her dog looked just like Lassie on T.V. and that was her real name, too. Of course, she **wasn't** the Lassie on T.V. but she sure could have been! Mary Francis loved that dog something fierce. I always figured it was because of the love she missed out on in other places in her life. Lassie followed her everywhere, if Mary Francis would let her, which she did most times. It was plain to see that Lassie loved Mary Francis near as much as Mary Francis loved Lassie. It was nice seeing how they were together. Mary Francis talked soft-like to Lassie, and Lassie looked up at her like that dog knew everything that she was saying. Lassie understood Mary better than nearly any other living creature except for me.

Mary Francis taught Lassie to do a few tricks, which she did real well. Lassie learned how to shake hands and play dead. That dog could do the "Play Dead" trick so well that she could get you to believing she was a goner, if you didn't know better. Other times, Lassie would sit up and beg which was her best trick and she did it whenever she met anyone. I always thought that Lassie probably wanted to show everyone what a smart dog she was at learning tricks. Even when Mary Francis was not speaking to anyone else in her family, and had barricaded herself in her bedroom by pushing her dresser or bed up against the bedroom door, it was a sure thing that Lassie was with her. No amount of coaxing could bring Mary to open the door, unless someone had the good sense to use the argument that Lassie was probably getting very thirsty and hungry. Even Mary Francis would cave in for that reason, if for no other at all. She sure loved that dog!

At our house no dogs were allowed. Mamma and Daddy could not abide having animals in the house. Mamma used to fuss that it was hard enough keeping a house clean with six people messing things up. Worrying about a critter running around, especially putting dirty paws down on a clean, black, shiny floor was more than she could tolerate. So, whenever Mary was at our house spending time, Lassie was usually laying on the floor of the garage watching the back door for any sign of Mary Francis to appear.

Daddy said it was, "Hard enough feeding six mouths and putting good food on the table without having to provide food for a d--- dog or cat!" Mamma would promptly change the subject and scold him proper, as she couldn't abide Daddy's use of "The language of a long shore-man," as she used to say. That translates into swearing for everyone else. You can see that having a pet like Lassie was definitely out for me, so I always paid particular attention to Lassie whenever she was around.

Mary would let me help brush or pick the burrs out of Lassie's long beautiful coat after returning from a tramp out to Saddle Canyon. Lassie always looked the most impressive after we had just finished brushing her out. Her long hair would hang shiny-smooth and all glittery-golden in the sunlight. I was fairly certain most of the other kids in the neighborhood were secretly jealous of Mary Francis having such a remarkable dog as Lassie. I loved to pretend that Lassie was half mine on account of Mary Francis and I being best friends, and Mary Francis let me. *Just like Timmy and his best friend, Porky, on the "Lassie" T.V. show: We sure loved that dog!*

Aside from the allowance grudge and having a beautiful dog like Lassie, Mary Francis got to have any kind of pop she wanted, anytime she wanted. Of course, Cherry Coke was her favorite, straight from her Daddy's soda fountain at the drugstore. Yep, anytime she finished a chore at the store, she'd get a tall glass of Cherry Coke with ice and a bendy straw for drinking it! Now that was the clincher! Me, being her best friend, I got one too, whenever we were together, but it was just the point of it all. Everybody else had to pay ten cents for a cherry coke with ice, and we got ours free just for sweeping the backroom and filling the ice machine with water. But paying customers didn't know that and we weren't offering up the information.

It was clear to me that Mary Francis got this every day and probably any candy bar of her choosing from one of the finest candy counters in town. Just seemed to me that life could be pretty good for ole' Mary Francis. The one big draw-back was the fact that she did have to go to the dentist a lot and get fillings in her teeth.

Mamma said, "Those frequent visits to the dentist are on account of her drinking all those Cherry Cokes and having candy always showing at the corner of her mouth. No other reason, and I won't have it! The Good Lord gives us pretty white teeth to shine and sparkle nice when we smile at others, and we best be taking good care of them and not turning them black and holey from drinking pop and eating too much candy." I guessed that I could see her point. It was true enough. The first sighting of baby teeth in most little mouths is a pleasing white peak.

Since my mamma was real strict on limiting pop and candy at our house, all those perks clearly weren't in the cards for me. I settled on being happy with any opportunity that presented itself, when in the company of Mary Francis. My little sisters kept themselves satisfied by sneaking candy from the Mary Francis Jar in our kitchen. Jackie and I would boost them up onto the cupboard. They would only take one piece so that Mamma wouldn't guess. Mamma had set that system up to protect Mary Francis from herself. Mamma would see those bulging pockets and call Mary Francis over to empty them out on the table. Mary got to keep her favorite piece, but the rest went in the Mary Francis Jar to save for another day. I thought it was interesting how that jar never seemed to get too full. I knew that it wasn't from my little sisters. They would only take one piece a day, and Mary Francis's pockets always held multiple pieces of candy, every day. You would have thought that after a while a bigger jar would be needed, but it never happened. *Puzzling...*

Chapter Eight

Leggins

As I look back to then, from my station today,
It was really quite funny, I must honestly say,
How that name I once dreaded has now come to be,
A name that is personally pleasing to me.
It marks out a time in my life that was good,
And leaves me with longing for days when I could...
Be different, be simple, be tolerant, kind.
And seldom be cold, and learn not to mind.

When it came to keeping a spotless house, you sure couldn't say my mamma wasn't clean! She spent every day, all day, with her bucket of ammonia and Spic'n'Span making every room in our little house sparkle. Grandma Jackson was always proud of the way Mamma kept the house so tidy and neat. As a satisfied mother, Grandma would take a long, slow look around, and say with a smile, "Yes Sir, cleanliness is next to Godliness...never can fault a clean house!" Both

Mamma and Grandma ran a pretty tight ship when it came to keeping a house. Even Mary Francis had to learn early on that shoes came off in the breezeway or on the porch before entering our house. We had the strictest of house rules on that matter!

All of the kids in the neighborhood played outside most every day. Playing inside the house was only for days when it was pouring rain, too cold or snowy, or just plain miserable. The television was only on for short periods of the day. One of those times was just after school was out. Only if we had been good at school, did we get to watch the Mickey Mouse Club. Daddy and Mamma always liked to watch the news just after dinner. The television was never on during meals. Most families enjoyed a few hours of night time viewing together as a family. Mostly, kids were outside from morning until night on any day that allowed it. We liked it that way, and so did our mothers.

Mamma had a reputation for having one of the whitest washes in the neighborhood. It sure did appear that way to my three sisters and me, when we'd see it flapping in the breeze and drying in the sun, as it hung on our clotheslines in the backyard. It would nearly make your eyes start aching with the pure brightness if it. The sheets on our beds smelled just like outdoors itself most months of the year. After Mamma took them down from the line and put them back on our beds, we'd always hear her say, "There's nothing as heavenly as sleeping all night on clean, line-dried sheets!" I sure believed that.

Kids at a very young age knew that you never touched clean sheets drying on the clothesline, unless you wanted some big trouble from the mom who hung them there. I remember one of the not so good days for the Carson kids. They decided to use their mother's clean sheets from the clothesline to make tents on the screened-in porch!

Daddy said, "It was like fireworks on the Fourth of July when Ruth Carson got home that day!" He had heard Mrs. Carson's sharp words and the protesting sobs of Mary Francis from the open porch, as he sat on the back step taking off his boots. He warned all of his little girls with a smile against shenanigans of that sort!

Mary wasn't allowed to play outside for three whole days! I thought that punishment would never end! I had to settle for playing with my younger sisters for almost a week. Mamma made sure it was clear to me and my little sisters, never to do such a thing as to make a tent out of clean sheets from the line without asking. She didn't have to tell us twice on that subject!

The kids on the block were in and out of the others' houses and yards on a regular basis. We were all part of the neighborhood gang and seemed "stuck together at the hip," as Grandpa liked to say. Even so, we did get into tangles from time to time.

We each had our own little irritations that would rub one or the other the wrong way. That was especially true on real hot, sticky August days. Occasionally the scrappin' and sassin' would reach to a knock-down, drag-out, free-for-all. It usually started out with friendly enough wrestling that turned, too rough. The families would start siding up sister to sister, sister to brother, brother to brother...family versus family. We'd start putting on strict rules concerning coming onto one or the other's property. We'd take to calling names and pointing out each's shortcomings, like who was always eating something which was probably directly related to their over-sized middle, or who always was thinking they were the 'Boss' which they were **not**! We'd get on to whose mamma was prettiest and whose daddy was the richest and whose upbringing was deserving of the most praise and who had bad manners like burping out loud or worse. *You know what I mean!*

We would go on like that for quite a while, as our voices got louder and louder. When the hollering reached a crescendo pitch... and it never took long... out would come the mothers of the warring factions. They'd shake their fingers and scowl at us, chattering together, with hands on hips. Taking turns they'd sternly declare,

"You are NOT to be playing with each other for three days!" one would start.

"Including: NO talking over property lines," the next mother doled out.

"NO calling on the phone or gazing lonesome-eyed out the windows," another hissed.

"AND, absolutely NO walking past each other's houses!" came another penance.

"There had better be NO waving for the other to come out," said one of the moms sternly.

"And THAT is THAT! Don't forget it! Everyone home in five minutes!" came the final judgment from yet another furious mother.

Usually with that said, they would turn on their heels and head for the house without so much as a glance back to see how we were receiving those instructions. Those sentences passed out in generous portions, meant long days of boredom and thinking about what it had been that started it all in the first place. Still, it didn't seem to keep us from it in the future. We managed to find trouble in other places, too.

Our neighborhood school was only a few walking minutes away from all our houses, so we lived a sheltered way of life. Robert Kerr School only had one classroom for every grade kindergarten through fifth. There were two elementary schools in town. We started kindergarten together, and stayed together every year until junior high school rolled around. Even when both of the elementary schools finally blended together in junior high, we still knew each other well from all the family ties, summer park programs, summer camps, swimming lessons at Meyers Lake, Boy and Girl Scout troops, and church activities. Living in a small town you are bound to know just about everyone.

Boys just naturally seem to enjoy teasing girls. Mary Francis and I just couldn't figure it out. Why was teasing always so much fun for them? I worked hard at learning not to mind the teasing so much. But no matter the season, even in the warmest of months, still that nickname of Leggins was a pressure point for me: All because of those gray woolen snow-pants that I wore every day the temperature was near freezing. When you lived in Michigan, leggings were necessary, on many more days than anyone cared to count.

Some of the girls had switched to the more stylish leg-tights, cute but not so warm. I begged for the new tights, but Mamma would have none of it. "Leggings are made to keep you warm. I'll not have you catching your death of pneumonia on account of not being dressed warm enough, when cold bitter days come along!" Mamma always had the last word on the wearing of the leggings. Just like there was no discussion about saddle shoes being worn to school every single day! No cutie bows or straps allowed! "Sensible shoes make for healthy feet," was Mamma's usual reply to our frequent complaints.

I loved poetry, and its sing-song rhythm. My teacher loved to read it, and I loved to hear it. I memorized poems all the time, and went about reciting them just for fun. I had quite a collection which I could draw from, upon request. One of my favorites was called "Choosing Shoes", by Ffrieda Wolfe. It was probably one of my favorites due to the ritual of wearing those saddle shoes. Regardless of the reason, one night, after an especially hard day of teasing going to and from school, sleep was coming hard. The darkness found me lying in bed with the usual playback of teasing drumming in my brain. My temper started to rise just thinking of it!

Why did they have to continually keep at it so relentlessly? Why were those gray woolen snow pants so worthy of the never-ending picking and teasing that was heaped on me day after day? If only Grandma would make them less bulky and more form fitting. Snow pants with something fancy or decorative and more interesting: NO more fat pants! Maybe then those pesky boys would STOP their annoying sing song words! The words came spilling out with anger, as I started **my** song of poetry; my heart and head telling the tale that I had longed to pour out for far too long.

Leggins

"Here comes Leggins," a familiar chant,
Wearing my gray, wooly, cozy snow pants.
Threadbare, frayed knees,
from play and hard use,
Through Michigan's winters
of snow and abuse.

Pull them on quickly, then button them tight,
Covered up warm for a cold snowball fight.
Or walking to school at fifteen below,
 Leggins it was, that battled the snow.

They kept me quite warm,
bundled toes to the chin,
And kept out the cold and the
chills from the wind.

TERESA LEE

If only the boys hadn't carried on so,
I think I'd have liked them much
more, don't you know?

With their teasing relentless,
as I came up the walk,
My leggings the brunt of
their sassy, smart talk.
I promised myself with a set to my jaw,
This would not continue, that was my law!

Some girls were more lucky and
wore pretty leg tights,
Brown, black or blue, maybe
pink...but not white.
At recess they huddled by
the door, all half froze,
With the leggings I wore, all
that stung was my nose.

Yet, I looked on those tights
with a longing remorse,
What could I do, to re-chart this sad course?
Of having to wear those
gray pants every day,
And endure, while the boys
carried on in this way.

I begged at my mom, and pleaded with Dad,
"Get rid of the leggings,
could that be so bad?
They're tattered and torn, a hole in the knee,
The boys in my school make fun out of me!"

But "NO" was the answer when
you're in third grade,

And don't have a voice, or
a choice to be made.
I guess my real reason...
I should have made clear,
Since Christmas that year,
was drawing quite near.

I hated those pants. I was a cartoon...
With pants fat enough to
slide over my boots,
Those boys never missed a
chance to shout out,
"Hey Leggins, please tell, what
are THOSE pants about?!!!"

A beautiful gift and a tag with my name
Was under the tree, the one I would claim,
And open with happy, excited delight.
A present my parents thought was just right.

Grandma had made them
from soft woolen yarn
And hid them 'til Christmas
outside in the barn.
Her eyes were alight when I opened the box,
And showed off the leggings
with matching gray socks.

"New leggings, how lovely,"
I said with despair.
As chatter of "Wonderful" filled up the air.
"Wonderful" wasn't the
word I would choose,
As I held them above the tops of my shoes.

TERESA LEE

"Mamma said that you needed
some new ones, My Dear.
Since yours have shown wear
since I made them last year,
I fashioned some new ones,
I hope you will like,
They will keep you quite warm
on your ride home tonight."

So, smiling I accepted my
fate with full grace,
Only wonder and gratefulness
showed on my face.
My mind filled with visions
of name-calling dread,
Since the boys that I knew still
had rocks in their heads.

To Robert Kerr School I
trudged with a smile,
With new gray knit leggings, lined
with pink for some style,
And tiny pink ribbons tied smartly in bows,
And all of the girls asking,
"Where'd you get those?
We love them! We want some
exactly the same!"
 Suddenly I felt like I'd just won the game!

Thank you, dear Grandma,
thank you so much,
I don't have to listen to teasing and such.
The boys even seem to think
these are grand,
You solved all my problems
with love, and your hand.

LEGGINS

That very Christmas my song of poetry changed. *Did I ever say these words out loud in my sleep? How did Grandma know what was in my heart?* Things definitely turned out better than I expected. After that Christmas, Mary Francis didn't have to defend me quite so ferociously. Just knowing that I had a pair of 'Cutie tights' calmed things down. The older boys at their safety posts seemed to change their constant bantering to a more once-in-awhile thing. They always called me Leggins, even in the hall at school, but it seemed softer and more endearing as the years went by. Who knew if they remembered what my real name was? Kids just seemed to recognize the nickname and use it more often than I cared to have them. I guess I was finally getting used to it, and felt that it wasn't all bad.

One thing was for sure about those leggings. When the wind blew and the snow flew at recess, I was always warmer than most of the other girls. My legs did not have to endure that intense redness and icy cold sting after being pelted with snowballs on the way home from school after a good snow had fallen. Nor did my legs, safe and snug under my snow pants, have to endure the bite of a frigid north wind that blew relentlessly through those very thin but stylish cutie tights.

Mary Francis proudly proclaimed, "Thank goodness for our Fat Pants! We enjoy more peace and quiet than those girls with the cutie tights! Who wants all those pesky boys around all the time anyway?"

We thought that tight circle of boys around those cutie tights was mostly to keep the girls who wore them from freezing to death before the bell rang (our welcomed signal to come back in the warm school). Mary and I usually lined up at the end of the line, with smiles on our faces and without chattering teeth, dressed in our warm woolen leggings. Hers red and mine gray.

All those girls in the cutie tights were huddled around the door, desperate to go into the warmth waiting just behind the closed door. We both agreed that warm and cozy was preferable to cute and freezing on most any winter day, especially when it came to cutie tights.

Chapter Nine

Private Property

Finding people who are treasures isn't always easy. Most of us have a less than attractive side, which sometimes makes it hard for others to see the beautiful part of our character. That fact is especially true when a temper tantrum or less than friendly attitude is thrown into the mix. First impressions are sometimes misleading.

Most of the time when you're looking for someone you can trust you will choose a person who has a soft easy smile or maybe someone who is friendly and easy to talk to in a quiet way. You don't usually choose the loud mouth in the corner who continues to lean their chair back against the wall, after having been warned for the tenth time by the scout leader, church choir director, or teacher. Who needs trouble like that? It never hurts to be picky. Least ways that's what Mary Francis and I had figured out.

The neighborhood kids thought it comfy and a bit uppity living where we did. Our addresses had a drive or avenue on the end. Not just the common street or road, like most people had in their addresses. Also, many of our fathers owned their own businesses or ran one and most of the grownups in town knew them. They went to meetings of the Masons, the Rotary, the City Council, the V.F.W., and sat on boards of churches and other local organizations.

After discussing these facts between us, the kids having prominent dads thought it really wasn't fitting to be flaunting such good fortune in front of anybody else's nose. We'd best keep it to ourselves and talk about it just when we were together. When I mentioned our agreement to Daddy I got the most surprising reaction! He slapped his leg, threw his head back, laughing 'til he nearly had a fit! I figured it must be on account of him liking that idea about keeping it to ourselves. It took him a while to settle down, but not to have his say.

As he finished wiping tears from his eyes due to his laughing, daddy added in a most serious tone, "Don't you kids get all full of yourselves. We are just regular folks... same as everybody else on this good earth. It would do all of you some good to keep that thought in mind!" *I always try to remember Daddy's words.*

All kids have disagreements now and then. Even though our neighborhood tribe of five to twelve-year-olds disagreed with each other from time to time, we were real protective of each other. Especially, when anybody from outside the neighborhood stirred up trouble or picked on one of our gang. Dale Hensley had that bad misfortune one day. He didn't soon forget it, and neither did we.

Dale Hensley was in the habit of wandering all over town. His mamma never seemed to know or care exactly where his adventures were taking him. It was known by most folks that his daddy had left years before. The story was that Jed Hensley had hopped a boxcar to Detroit. His leaving had left Dale's mamma working seven days a week at the diner in East Town. She tried as best she could to raise two boys all by herself, living in a run-down, rickety house behind the foundry. Dale was always looking for a fight. I was for certain sure it was due to not having his dad around and being deep down hurt. Dale was just plain mad about the whole idea of his dad taking off and leaving the family to fend for themselves.

Sure enough, on one particular hot August day here came Dale Hensley strolling up the street with his black hair straight and pokey and looking like it needed a proper washing. His thick wide eyebrows were squinched down tight above his hard steely dark eyes. It was clear enough to anybody within seeing distance that he was bent on some kind of meanness. Mary Francis didn't help his mood.

"We-e-ell... just lookie what the cat dragged in!" she crowed.

Dale stopped short and glared at Mary Francis. He wouldn't take her on! She had knocked him down and washed his face in snow just last February, when Dale had yanked the hood on my coat and choked me. Nobody messed with Mary Francis, not even Dale Hensley, 'cuz you just never knew what she was going to do! Mary Francis was our very own ticking time bomb, and her parents' very own personal firecracker!

"Who invited you into this neighborhood?" she continued.

Conrad Douglas was picked out to be Dale's target that day. Thinking back, it was probably due to his mamma having dressed him in freshly ironed, clean, white shorts. Sunny knee socks matched his bright yellow shirt. Dale totally ignored Mary Francis' stabs.

Dale Hensley started right in, "No real boy ever dresses like that, and has such clean fingernails all the time. You're just a Sissy!" He must have had a point since all the other boys standing around started looking at their nails, nodding their heads in agreement. Sure enough, dirt under every single one, except Conrad's. That didn't help at all! When Conrad saw all the other boys looking at their hands, plainly dirty and needing a good scrub, he started right in putting up a major fuss. He was yelling something awful, on account of Dale suggesting he wasn't a real boy. It wasn't the first time Conrad and Dale had come to blows!

Dale saw his chance right off for really heating things up and began picking on Dotty Douglas, Conrad's sister. With a nasty smirk on his face he began to tease, "Dotty, do you wear polka dot underpants to match yer name, 'cuz I heard a rumor that ya' did?"

All the kids standing around listening to Dale's insults sucked in their breath at that suggestion. Next, Dale started in comparing Dotty Douglas to his great-grandmother, Ida, who in her old age had lost her mind. Most warm days Grandma Ida just sat all day on the porch rocking back and forth staring straight ahead, not saying anything to anybody.

"Yep, you must be witless just like her 'cuz mom says she's **dotty**," Dale continued with his barbs. Then right out loud, that snarly Dale Hensley challenged, "Yes Sir, it's a sure bet that **Dotty** Douglas probably can't even spell her own name on account of havin' no brains."

The fireworks started when Dotty burst into tears! Before Dale Hensley knew what happened, Conrad slammed him square in the mouth with his doubled up fist and clean white fingernails.

TERESA LEE

Dale was more surprised than anything else. When he drew his hand back from his mouth there was blood dripping from his fingers in a steady stream. His front tooth was completely gone and his lip had a fearsome looking gash. Every kid witnessing Conrad's unexpected charge, gasped in unison as the blood ran down Dale Hensley's chin. You couldn't help but notice through his sneer: A large obvious hole, stood dark and empty, where his tooth used to be. Dale bent over like he was looking around for that missing tooth and quick as a wink, plunged head first right into Conrad. Both went down hard. Conrad was on the bottom side of the pile and squealing like a roped pig. Conrad continued to kick and punch at his attacker. Dale was roaring mad now and started pounding on poor Conrad. The blood, still gushing from Dale's mouth, was dripping all over Conrad's bright yellow shirt and white shorts. Conrad's matching knee socks were covered with grass stains and dirt. Nothing about that outfit matched now! And only moments ago from head to toe it had all looked so fresh and clean.

I never knew exactly when the other boys decided that enough was enough. The Nelson brothers had been the first to put a stop to the fight. Denny Nelson gave Dale Hensley a tongue lashing while his older brother and the other boys restrained Dale's swinging fists.

"We'll have no bullies in our neighborhood!" Denny declared as he grabbed the front of Dale's bloodied shirt and pulled him off from Conrad. "The next time you need to satisfy that mean streak you carry around, you best do it somewhere else!" he finished with a shove. The other boys gathered around started the task of showing Dale the way out of the neighborhood. Like a one-sided game of Tug of War, we stood and watched them drag Dale Hensley kicking, punching and screaming all the way to the corner at the end of the street. I guess he figured that all those boys had him outnumbered. By the time they reached the perimeter of our neighborhood, the fight had gone out of Dale, and no one had raised another fist to him. He sat where the boys plunked him down. On the sidewalk, now quiet, still mad, he sported a missing tooth, a bloody face, and stained shirt.

Conrad and Dotty had immediately disappeared into their house, on the heels of tears and promises of getting even. Both stayed there the rest of that day. Mrs. Douglas appeared suddenly on the porch, just as Dale was being escorted to the curb. She stood there staring hard, with a stink-eye glare, at a very dejected Dale Hensley, sitting alone on the curb, head in hands. I guess she thought better of saying anything to him, because she just turned around and walked back inside the house. It seemed that the lesson had been learned: Bullies were off limits on Dartmouth Drive.

Mary Francis and I thought it a good thing that none of our mothers had been around to hear the long buzz of cussing that had come from such a stirred up beehive of boys. Every mom would have had something serious to say about that! Using 'profane language' was as bad as fighting when it came to what our dear mothers considered acceptable. How many times had we all heard one or all of them repeat, "If you can't say anything nice, don't say anything at all!" Another constant reminder they never tired of repeating. It was the same as using our "Please" and "Thank-you" to show proper manners every time it was required. Yep! Best that the moms weren't within earshot of that tangle.

We all made a pact that day. None of us would ever allow a hard-luck kid, from the other side of the tracks, to come into our neighborhood and hurt one of our friends while the rest stood by and watched, leastways

TERESA LEE

not without a fight! However, truth be told, we should have told our parents and let the adults handle it before it came to fists. There were no winners that day. Each had lost a bit of something in the fray.

Dale Hensley's front right tooth never did grow back. Conrad Douglas sported a black eye for several weeks afterward, as testimony to one of his more memorable rites of passage toward manhood. Knowing that he was responsible for Dale's tooth being gone, Conrad decided that wearing any sort of sock that rose above mid-leg wasn't fitting attire for a real boy. He never wore knee socks again. It was a very long time before Dale Hensley came back into our neighborhood looking for trouble. *No surprise there.*

Chapter Ten

Sweet Revenge

A real treasure can sometimes be mixed up with a lot of junk that has to be sorted out. Friends can be like that, too. They come from all different kinds of families. Some families have problems. Stressful family troubles and life stories can get in the way of your ability to see the true value of a person's worth. The precious spirit that is everyone's gift can get covered over with years of sorry days and sleepless nights. It may take a while before you realize that you've found that perfect treasure in a certain friend. It's rather like wearing sunglasses inside the house. Things can appear shaded and harder to see. The trick is to take off those dark glasses and keep looking right to the heart of the matter. The light suddenly dawns, the darkness disappears and you see things so much clearer. Mary Francis and I discovered that together.

I figured that "having each other's back" was sort of like when Mary Francis socked Dale Hensley good and proper, because he pulled the hood on my coat and choked me. I must admit that doing the "Friends for Life Blood Pact", in Mary's basement, did require some blood-letting. Not to worry though! We used small needles and afterward drowned our wounds in Merthiolate, while the other blew really fast on the stinging wound, and slapped on a polka-dot Band-Aid. We were pledged to be each other's protectors, so there was no choice in the matter.

I was always a bit afraid of Dale Hensley, especially after witnessing his brawl with Conrad Douglas. Also because rumor had it that Dale was friendly with Boxcar Joe! Most kids in town were scared silly of Boxcar Joe. He was a strange character who lived in town and drifted about with no rhyme or reason. Some of the neighbor boys had seen Dale Hensley talking to Joe on the street one day. They shared how amazing it was that Dale didn't seem one bit afraid of Old Joe. Dale Hensley had some grit that was for sure! No other kid ever even thought about talking to Boxcar Joe.

Over time, I made it a point of always being extra nice to Dale Hensley, smiling kindly whenever he was about. *Better to be a friend than an enemy of this guy.* I guess my plan worked, because over the course of third grade, he became my walk-to-school guardian. On many days when it was time to leave for school, there he would be, standing on the sidewalk in front of my house waiting for my sister and me to come out. Mary Francis got mad sometimes and told him to leave us alone.

"What you doin' around here, Dale Hensley?" she would demand. "Hope you're not thinkin' on stirrin' up some trouble again!"

I said, "It's O.K., Mary. He just wants to walk to school with us."

Mary Francis snapped right back, "Who needs him, I can take care of us!"

This was absolutely true, because she could and had on several occasions. Remember the snow washing she gave Tommy Trundle? Even Dale was wary of Mary.

More than once Dale had gotten himself in trouble defending me. It was the same old routine with the Safety Patrol boys tormenting me on the way to school. They loved using their favorite tease of all, calling me "Leggins." *Yep, that same stupid nickname.* Dale had gone after one or another of those boys, on several occasions, until they quit the name-calling. That's how he got himself into trouble, one day in the spring of third grade. Dale Hensley had to sit in the principal's office most of the day. Mrs. Kurski called his mother and told her to keep Dale home the next day because of his fighting. Dale told Mary Francis and me that Mrs. K., our principal, had demanded that Dale learn to control his temper and stop the fighting. He and Mrs. K had gone through this before, so he promised to try and please her.

I worried less about Dale choosing me as a target after that. Someone else was usually the target if Dale was around and thought that I was not being treated kindly. He even pulled Mary Francis off from me one early spring day when she thought it would be funny to push me down and wash my face with snow. I was crying and that was all it took for Dale to fly into guardian mode. I never knew for sure if he was doing it for me, or to get even with Mary Francis for the snow washing she had given him the year before. After the face washing Dale gave her that day, she didn't do that again for a very long time, at least not when Dale was around! It occurred to me that even a bully has a soft side. You just have to keep looking. If only bullies understood; the true friendship they want so badly is often kept at a distance by their own hand. Bullies hurt themselves the most by what they say and do to others. Though anyway you looked at it, a bodyguard sometimes proved to be very advantageous, that means helpful, even when it came to your best friend.

I learned to appreciate Dale Hensley for many reasons other than my protection. Even though he had a reputation for being tough, he could be very considerate and even funny sometimes. I never once saw him act mean toward Toby Taylor. Of course, no one was ever mean to Toby anymore: Not since the train accident when Toby lost a leg and Boxcar Joe had saved his life. Dale always spoke kindly to Toby and offered to push the wheelchair whenever he got the chance. Toby let him and seemed to like the way Dale kept him safe and treated him like he was special. Dale enjoyed the time he spent with Toby. They always talked together in a relaxed and comfortable way. The two boys liked each other and enjoyed one another's company. Not many people could ever say that about Dale Hensley. You could tell that Toby liked Dale, but then Toby liked Boxcar Joe, too.

Whenever Dale showed his softer side, which was never in view of the older boys, his eyes didn't snap when you looked at him and he had a great smile, with a deep dimple in his left cheek, even though most people never saw it much. I thought that he probably didn't like to show it on account of his missing tooth. I liked to hear him laugh, which could have been counted on less than ten fingers for all the years I knew him. Even though he and Mary Francis didn't always see eye-to-eye on many things, she was one of the people who could really make him laugh. Ricky Grant was the other.

When Mary Francis and Ricky Grant went after each other, it could make anyone laugh. They never got on well, so that happened a lot. Dale seemed to think it was real funny whenever other people were in a tangle of some sort. Dale loved to recall one of the days he laughed the hardest, which always made him laugh again.

The weather had started to warm, finally. The Detroit Tigers were playing one of their first games of the season on Sunday. Most people would be watching on T.V., if they had one, or listening on the radio if they didn't. A number of the kids at school had agreed we'd team up and play a game of ball at the field on Saturday morning. Everyone was ready to celebrate spring and the opening of baseball season. A couple of the neighborhood dads had just mowed the field and set up the bases that week. Our baseball diamond was ready for play, whenever we chose to get a game going. Kids played baseball regularly, even the girls.

Dale Hensley had come by and two of the older boys asked him to play so the teams would be even. You could tell by the look on Dale's face that he was surprised by the invitation but liked the idea. He hadn't come into the neighborhood to play very often since the nasty disagreement between him and Conrad. He also probably didn't want to take the chance of getting a lecture from Mr. or Mrs. Douglas. Dale was chosen to be on Mary Francis' and my team.

Mary Francis and Ricky had been at each other all day. They knew how to push each other's buttons and did every chance they got. Ricky, R.G. for short, was still mad because Mary did not pick him to be on her team when we chose up sides for the game of ball we had going earlier that Saturday morning.

Mary's team won and of course, she rubbed it in, "That's why I didn't choose you, R.G. I wanted to win today." Ricky stuck out his tongue at Mary Francis, which by the way was covered with chewed up animal crackers, and she returned the favor. Hers was colored purple from the wad of grape bubble gum that she had been chewing. *Yuck!* When we teamed up to play Catch the Monkey, a game of chase that we liked to play, Ricky refused to choose Mary Francis even when she was the last one to be chosen. He went with one less on his team just out of spite.

She yelled, "Oh I see, getting even 'cuz I didn't pick you this morning for the ball game! Well, see if I let you ride my scooter to Saddle Canyon the next time you ask, you sore loser!"

Ricky countered with, "Well, see if I care one whit about your stupid scooter! Maybe I'll just ride your four-legged carnie dog. I have a saddle in my garage that would probably fit!"

Mary spun around with her back to R.G. but said nothing. Mary Francis could tolerate and persist in most teasing for a while, but not about her dog! Nobody said anything negative about Lassie. Dale looked at me with surprise and his eyes flew wide open as if to say what I was already thinking. *Oh no, here comes trouble!*

I was completely unprepared for what came next. She turned around with the sweetest smile on her face, as if she had not just heard what Ricky said about her beloved canine family member. Mary said to everyone gathered there, "Let's all go over to my house and have an ice cream cone. Mom just bought a new gallon of chocolate and said we could have cones for an afternoon treat." Ricky Grant loved ice cream of any flavor, but chocolate was definitely his favorite. Actually, no treat was ever refused by R.G. Well, Ricky G. fell for that invitation hook, line, and sinker. Not me, I knew something was up!

Mary Francis, with the help of her mother because it was a Saturday, served up the ice cream cones to everyone there. Ricky of course had to be last, because she was still mad at him. So, with great delight we had all started to slurp up the chocolate ice cream cones we had been served. Ricky waited patiently for the last cone to be dipped. Mary was dipping up the ice cream for the cone that was to be R.G.'s. Mrs. Carson had just finished the last one for Mary Francis, and handed it to her. Mary turned sweetly to her mother and said, "Mom, I can finish here, why don't you go inside and relax. Thanks for helping and letting us have an ice cream treat. This is fun!" *This was not typical Mary Francis.*

Almost as soon as the front door of their house closed behind her mother, Mary Francis turned to R.G. with the final cone in her hand and said in her most cordial voice, "Here Ricky G., enjoy your ice cream! The treat's on me!"

With that, she shoved that chocolate ice cream cone in Ricky Grant's face with great satisfaction. That was the day that we all watched Dale Hensley laugh 'til he cried, no apologies or excuses necessary. Everyone except Ricky G. started out laughing, even Mary Francis. However, everyone **except** Mary Francis was laughing at the end of this escapade. Brown ice cream smashed on Ricky's face was more than funny! Still, when it first happened, the surprise of it all caused us to draw a breath in unison.

R.G. looked like a raccoon. The expression on Ricky's face and his reaction was what was hilarious. What Mary Francis thought would be the worst thing she could possibly do to Ricky that day, to get even with him for calling her dog a four-legged carnival horse, turned out to be the very best part of R.G.'s entire day, maybe his whole week!

When the chocolate ice cream hit Ricky's face, he reacted with shock. His eyes flew open wide and he stood for a second, stunned from the cold thick goop on his face. It only took him an instant to decide that it felt pretty good on such a warm day, and would taste even better! He blew it out of his nose, into his hand, and licked it up like a cat drinking milk out of a saucer. He started licking his face, opening his mouth very wide and lapping it up like a clown. Ricky used his fingers to wipe off his face every bit he could get and then stick them, covered with ice cream, into his mouth.

Ricky G. relished every moment, sharing his further enjoyment of the unexpected treat with great exaggeration. That Ricky Grant had completely turned Miss Mary's ploy back on her. Everyone was rolling on the ground laughing. Mary Francis stood there glaring with rage at his antics, and the great satisfaction he was getting from all this attention. This had not turned out as she had hoped. "And don't you call my dog a 'carnie dog' ever, ever again!" She turned and stomped back into the house slamming the door shut behind her.

At that point, Ricky G. shrugged his shoulders, raised his eyebrows and softly quipped, "Touchy." We laughed even harder!

Mary Francis was not seen for the rest of that day. Ricky went home to wash off the remainder of the sticky sweet ice cream smeared on his face, so that the bees would not follow him around the rest of the day. Dale Hensley laughed and laughed that day and for many days to come at the mere mention of chocolate ice cream cones! It was interesting how R.G. never held that 'ice cream-in-the-face' episode against Mary Francis. Even more perplexing was that she never mentioned the whole ordeal even once in front of R.G. or his buddies. Things between Mary Francis and Ricky Grant didn't change much after that, but they weren't best enemies either.

Chapter Eleven

Surly Serpents

On warm summer days all the neighborhood kids would meet over in Nelson's field and plan how we would go out to Saddle Canyon that day. It was about a half mile or more of walking just to get back there. The going was not easy from the start, as the path went through empty lots and the dug up parts in the back of the subdivision. The route we took back to Saddle Canyon meandered through many weedy fields just waiting for new houses to be built there. As you got closer to the canyon, it was real hilly and lonesome back there, with little thickets of trees and tall thick grass. It was where we loved to play the most. It was where we spied on Boxcar Joe and the hobos who rode the rails.

It was easier walking if we followed the narrow grass trails where some of the townies (kids who live in the town area and know the surroundings well) rode motorbikes, and two wheelers. The local teenagers helped keep some of the open fields mashed down. Saddle Canyon was a favorite spot to park their cars and meet up with friends to party, without their folks knowing about it. We could tell what went on because of the beer bottles that were always lying about. It was a treasure trove for the hoboes and Boxcar Joe. They traded the empty bottles in for coins that they used to buy meals. It seemed real adventuresome being out there so far from home and knowing that if some terrible happening came up you'd have to be figuring it all out on your own. Saddle Canyon was too far away from our neighborhood to get help in a hurry.

One steamy afternoon after the Fourth of July, a bunch of us had decided it was too hot to trek back to the canyon. It was much more comfortable sitting in the shade of the willow tree in Mary Francis' side yard. So, Mary Francis, Jackie, and I were playing games of Jacks, Pick-up Sticks, and some of our favorite card games. Kris Kettle, Katie Cameron, Billy, Mickey, Rudy Keller, and other neighborhood kids had joined us. We were relaxed from the cool comfort of staying put under the tree. Instantly, Ricky Grant came speeding over on his bike, with the tail of his Davy Crockett coon-skin hat flying straight out behind him. Even on the hottest of days, he was always proudly wearing that ratty old raccoon fur hat. Most all the boys we hung out with surely loved Davy Crockett, and his frontiersmen friends.

Most days they could be heard singing or humming that theme song, "*Davy... Davy Crockett...King of the wild frontier,*". They were always going on about Davy fightin' the bears, and gettin' the bad guys. I was fairly certain that not one of those boys ever missed a single episode of that T.V. show, starring *Fess Parker as Davy Crockett*. With that raccoon hat covering one eye, R.G. screeched to a halt almost on top of our plate of peanut butter and apple jelly sandwiches that Mamma had made for a picnic lunch.

Ricky always knew when the grub was being served and never failed to show up at the first mention of eats. He carried around a constant state of the hungries and could smell food from a significant distance; hence his arrival. Even before eyeing the plate of his favorite sandwiches, his words came tumbling out, one over the other, until we all shouted for him to stop and start again.

"S...L...O...W...E...R.!" we all chimed, so R.G. began again.

He told the story about how Kris Stricker and his older brother, Kurt, had ridden their bikes back to Saddle Canyon this very morning and been chased by a huge blue racer snake. Ricky had experienced his own confrontation with a blue racer just the summer before, so snakes were still off his list of friendly critters! Following is R.G.'s calmer version of the snake caper.

Kris and Kurt had gone back to Saddle Canyon searching out arrowheads. Kris had thrown the chain on his bike and gotten off to fix it. Kurt, not knowing, had gone on ahead without looking back. When Kurt finally did a head check and saw that Kris wasn't coming he turned and started back for him, wondering what was keeping his younger brother. Kurt was almost back to where he thought Kris had stopped, when suddenly Kris started screaming like the devil was on his tail.

Kurt came to a screeching halt, tires skidding to the point of nearly knocking him off his bike. It took a few seconds for the dust to settle. Kurt's eyes were riveted to the horrific look on his brother's face. He followed the line to Kris' steady stare. Kurt's mouth went dry as he stared at the biggest snake he had ever seen. A gigantic beady eyed serpent was peering right up into his little brother's ashen face. Kris was still holding on to his bicycle chain, crouched down on his knees, with his back as stiff as a three day starched shirt. Neither one dared to move on account of not knowing what that cagey blue racer was thinking on doing. Kris just stood there staring down that snake.

The younger brother was clearly terrified. In a shaking voice he pleaded, "Kurt, are these the ones that bite or the ones that crawl like lightning up your pant leg? What should I do?!"

Kurt hissed in a whispered voice, "Well, for one thing S-H-H-H, BE quiet! STOP talking!" The poor critter started to make his move at raisin' his head up real high to have a better look around, as its tongue flicked in and out at lightning speed. That action must have broken the spell that Kris was under.

With his continuous piercing scream of "RUN-N-N!" Kris threw his disabled bike on top of that blue racer. Jumping sideways of the squirming serpent he bolted onto the back of Kurt's bike. It happened like a flash, all in one motion, or so it seemed to Kurt. No one had to be telling him what to do next! Kurt pushed off and pedaled till his heart was thumping like the valve of a pressure cooker on high heat.

With not one thought of stopping to look back to see if that blue racer was on their heels, Kurt never let up until his bike wheels were back on the first black-topped road in the subdivision. At two blocks away from the spot where it all happened, Kris mustered the courage to look back. No blue racer. Kurt put on the brakes and both boys stopped to gasp for breath as the sweat poured off their foreheads, dripped down their noses, and soaked the backs of their short-sleeved shirts. Ricky had seen them fly by with no greeting. That never happened, so he knew something big was up! He ran a full block to catch them and see what all the commotion was about.

Later that afternoon, Mrs. Stricker had sent her sons' pa back, with his truck, to get Kris' bike. The blue racer was gone, but neither Kris nor Kurt would have known for themselves, since their dad went alone and followed the map Kris and Kurt had drawn. Mr. Stricker could see real plain from the crayon map, where the bike could be found, along with probably the biggest and hopefully deadest snake any dad ever saw. No dead snake, just a flattened bike in a clearly trampled area of weeds along the trail that went back to Saddle Canyon. Ricky was certain it was the very same varmint that had chased him the summer before. Yes Sir-r-ee... going to Saddle Canyon was off the list again for R.G., at least for a while!

Ricky Grant ended his mesmerizing story with, "So, neither of the Stricker boys will be getting up the nerve to visit Saddle Canyon anytime soon."

Denny and Dale Nelson, who had been listening to R.G.'s story most intently, both admitted, "Yep, we've seen blue racers in the grass along the trail. Just last week, Tommy Trundle got chased by a smaller one as we were all coming back from Saddle Canyon. That snake was right on his heels most of the way out!"

The rest of us were very relieved to hear that the snakes seen had been small enough not to be worrisome. Just in case, it was agreed that we would all be on the lookout for anything slithering in the tall grass. It was also firmly decided: Probably best if trips to the canyon were put on hold at least for a little while. *No argument there!*

It was so nice sitting under the willow tree eating peanut butter and jelly sandwiches, and sipping our ice cold, cherry Kool-Aid. Saddle Canyon would still be there waiting for us after things simmered down with the blue racers. On that we all agreed. Just sharing a warm summer afternoon and talking about all of our plans for when we did make the hike over to Saddle Canyon was enough for the moment. We were all content after R.G.'s story to just let those blue racers have their way for a while and we would all steer clear of those tall trail grasses that lined the way to Saddle Canyon. Strange how best intentions like that never lasted long.

Gratefully moving the conversation away from nasty snakes, and bringing up other scary possibilities, Mary Francis had to point out, that in addition to those pesky snakes, there was always the chance of being caught in Saddle Canyon all alone and running into Boxcar Joe. Now that was something to make your blood run cold. Boxcar Joe was a loner type in our town. A real character, who our mammas said, we should not cross paths with. You never could tell what Ole' Joe was up to or what your fate might be if you were unlucky enough to meet up with him and have nobody else around. He was always totin' that burlap bag with who knew what in it. Mary Francis set us all straight on the fact that he sometimes used that old burlap bag to pick up beer bottles he found laying about out there. He brought them to her dad's drugstore and was paid three cents on a bottle.

Still, who knew? He might even use it for the purpose of kidnapping some poor little child with the bad misfortune of being all alone in Saddle Canyon. It wouldn't take more than a second of having been separated from your gang to get snatched! Boxcar Joe was seen out there occasionally and with all the wild stories running around town about him, you just never could tell. And what about those hobo friends that he had a habit of hanging around with? Taken altogether, they were an interesting bunch!

Mary Francis and I had spent the better part of one afternoon watching Joe drag an old burlap bag around

TERESA LEE

the canyon. We had laid on our bellies, just outside one of our forts, watching his every move. Our imaginations, about what he might have in that bag, got the better of us. We headed for home pronto, especially after we thought he looked our way and spied us, spying on him. A kid just couldn't be too careful with somebody like Boxcar Joe skulking around.

After a spell of talking it out, we most generally decided to play the rest of the afternoon at having a ball game or starting a card game, like Crazy Eights, right in our own neighborhood within seeing distance of our houses. (*The future would give us a kinder understanding of Old Joe, but, that's another story...*)

Chapter Twelve

The Tuberculosis Sanatorium

When people in your life get sick, it is a very scary time. You worry about everything, and think that this is the worst thing that could ever happen to you, and sometimes it is, but more often it turns out okay. The real important thing to remember when you are going through a hard time, is that other people around you love you and want you to know it. When people you know are going through a hard time, that's when you show your love and reach out. It makes them feel better, and it makes you feel good, too. Living through tough days with Mary Francis taught me that.

Mary Francis had a real nice house. It was big too, bigger than ours with fewer people living there. Mr. Carson, being a store owner, made good money.

"He's bringing home the bacon," Daddy liked to say.

This allowed her mamma to hire a housekeeper. "Just once a week to come in and help with the chores that never seem to get finished," Mrs. Carson explained, giving her reason for the housemaid. "Every day is so busy working at the store, those things around the house just don't get done properly."

I knew for sure that my Mamma would have enjoyed that luxury once in a while, but stay-at-home moms just did the work themselves. Mostly, it cost too much to have a housekeeper, but then, the Carsons could afford it.

Mary Francis had her very own room with two beds and matching bedspreads. She had her very own desk with a white milk-glass lamp. It had a purple fabric lampshade, which was Mary's favorite color. In the corner of her room sat a big rocking chair covered with quilt-like fabric made from big bright multi-colored squares, especially for her own use. Rocking seemed to calm Mary Francis down when she was in one of her moods. She would start out rocking it as fast as it would go, sometimes banging the wall over and over, if her parents weren't at home. Gradually it would rock slower and slower and soon her smile would be back, with the previous irritations forgotten, at least for the moment.

Paul had his own room with everything the same as Mary Francis, but decorated more for a boy, with the walls painted in forest green, khaki and blue. At our house, two sisters shared a room with two twin beds. No extra rocking chairs or desks, because there was only enough room for a chest of drawers. We never minded sharing a room, because we liked talking to someone before we drifted off to sleep. I always wondered if Mary Francis missed that. Whenever she stayed the night she was still whispering long after my sisters were asleep.

Life could become instantly interesting when the Carson parents backed their big Buick Electra out of the driveway and drove away, on their way to another day of work. It was like opening the door of Grandma Cole's birdcage. Oh my, what freedom that offered for the little birds that lived inside. Just like those

TERESA LEE

beautifully feathered parakeets that responded to the open door, the fun for the day was just about to begin. Despite the sitter that came on some days when Mary Francis and Paul found themselves home on a regular school day or over vacation time, still they managed to find some mischief to get into. Of course, they always waited for the right moment to begin.

It was no secret that many people smoked cigarettes. That habit was a fact of life. Grandpa explained, "So many people smoking' cigarettes is probably on account of the rations on cigarettes during World War II. The government was real strict on that. Two packs a week, period. No more than two, was all they would allow any one askin' for 'em. That would probably be the reason you see so many more folks smokin' one cigarette after another. Sad state of affairs I'd say!"

Mary Francis and Paul liked to raid the kitchen drawer where their parents kept the cigarettes. Now you would think that a certified nurse and a druggist would be the last people lighting up cigarettes, on account of the habit being bad for your health and stinky, too! Nope, both of them were chain smokers. Between them, they smoked a pack a day; twenty cigarettes, ten each. When they weren't working, they spent most of the day with a cigarette in their mouth: mowing the lawn, puffing; cleaning the house, puffing; making the salad for dinner, puffing; watching the evening news with John Cameron Swasey, still puffing.

No wonder Mary Francis wanted to play outside all the time. She hated being inside the house breathing in all that smoke. And yet, when Mary and Paul wanted to get their day off to a mischievous start, they went right to that cigarette drawer. One pulled out an open cigarette pack, sliding out a cigarette for each of them. The other grabbed the matches and both headed for the basement, with Mary Francis pulling on my hand to follow. My protestations stated my intent to never touch one of those dreadful things to my lips. They never asked why. Hearing my reasons, wasn't a popular topic. They knew what I said was true. Paul always called me a "Daddy's girl," and I didn't even care!

The fruit cellar was the place where Mary Francis and Paul always went to light up. Most Michiganders having basements had a small room called a fruit cellar where they kept fruits and vegetables cool in the summer and stored for the winter. Behind the fruit cellar door you could find shelves of canned jars that held all the best from the fall harvest. Beans, beets, tomatoes, pickles, pears, and all sorts of other home canned goods colored the room. Baskets of potatoes, onions, apples, squash and other needed foods waited there for use. By the looks of the Carson's fruit cellar, it appeared that Mr. C. got paid in canned goods when families, down on their luck, couldn't pay for needed medicines or other things they purchased at the drug store. I knew Mrs. Carson was way to busy to can that much food in a season. It was a room for storage, not smoking!

Mary Francis and Paul would pretend to be all grown up, holding their cigarette the way people on the street do. They'd mimic their mom and dad and the way they would sit at the breakfast table, enjoying their first smoke of the day. With so much practice, they had it down to a near perfect act. I hated it when they did that. I just knew that their parents would come walking in the door any minute, and smell the smoke rolling up the basement stairs. If they got an unexpected call from their parents saying that they'd be home for lunch, or be home in a minute to pick something up that they needed, Mary Francis would fly up the stairs for the aerosol spray can from the bathroom and give the basement a good dose to hide their mischief.

Personally, I never knew a Michigan basement to smell like Lily-of-the-Valley in January!

Mary Francis and Paul didn't seem to be one bit afraid of getting caught.

"Oh, don't get so worked up!" Paul snarled at me. "All they ever do is send us to our room and say 'No dessert for either of you'!" he mimicked.

Mary Francis quickly agreed, "I don't care one fig about what we're having for dessert tonight! What's so great about Orange Sherbet anyway?" she pouted. "Not even a cookie to go with it! Who cares?" With anger she took another puff on her cigarette.

I knew for sure that Mamma and Daddy would tan my backside good and proper if they knew that I was a party to 'such shenanigans' even if I didn't take one single puff on a cigarette. Grandpa Jackson had quit smoking when I was three years old, after continual nagging from Mamma and Grandma J. He never did smoke in the house. No smoking ever at Grandma and Grandpa Cole's house, because Grandma Cole would have none of it. She was fussy about having a clean house and couldn't abide the smell or the yellow film on walls, windows and ceilings that smoking left behind. Smoking was not something that happened in my house or in my grandparents' houses. Lots of people smoked, just no one in our family.

One particular morning, shortly after the smoking had started, I took my usual cue to head for home, because it was certain that Paul and Mary Francis didn't care how long they stayed down in the fruit cellar, or even if their parents came home and caught them. Playing around like that was not something I wanted my parents to know that I was doing. I didn't want Mr. or Mrs. Carson telling my parents that I was a party to any of this behavior. They would have been very disappointed in the fact that I was taking part in something our whole family chose not to do.

As soon as I was out the door, I started flapping my arms and running around in my own backyard to make sure that all that smoky smell was off my clothes before I went in the house and faced Mamma. She could smell cigarette smoke a block away, and sure enough, this day was to be no different.

"Young lady, where have you been?" She quizzed the minute I walked in the door. "You smell like a smoke factory!"

"Hi, Mamma. I've been over at Mary Francis' house."

"Well I know for a fact that Arden and Ruth have been gone to work for over an hour! Open your mouth wide and breathe out," she commanded as she stooped over, stuck her nose just in front of my open mouth within close inspection range.

I did as I was told, as Mamma took in a deep sniff of my breath. She stood up with her hands on her hips and looked squarely in my eyes.

"I'm proud that you did right, Sweetie. Don't ever come home with cigarette smoke on your breath." I never did.

Mamma knew how Mr. and Mrs. Carson smoked, but it didn't make us like them any less. We all were real partial to the whole family. We just held different views when it came to smoking. After that day, Mamma just made me run around some more and take my sweater and shoes and socks off in the breezeway before I came in the house. Mamma would just look down, at my discarded clothes lying on the garage floor, draw in a deep breath and not say anything. I knew the words were inside her head, and going to stay there.

When Mary Francis and I were in second grade, things changed for the worse at the Carson's. Mr. C contracted Tuberculosis, a disease of the lungs that was highly contagious. After a day long trip to the hospital, in one of the biggest cities in our area, we got the news that he would have to go to a Tuberculosis sanatorium for almost a year. That's a place where a very sick person has to stay all the time until cured. They can't go home at all. The family can visit only once a week. Everyone has to wear masks and keep their distance. I couldn't imagine how sad it would be if you couldn't hug or kiss your daddy every day! It made my eyes tear up just thinking of what was in store for Mary!

Mr. Carson's stay at the sanatorium was not going to be a good thing for the family or the business. He immediately began wearing a mask around the house and at the store. Mrs. Carson cried for three days. Mamma took dinners over and kept Mary Francis at our house until things got figured out and settled down. Mr. Carson would be going away for many months.

One evening, a few days before he was to leave for the T.B. Sanatorium, Mr. Carson came over and spoke quietly to my parents in our kitchen. Jackie and I were supposed to be in our beds, but we were hiding just around the corner behind the desk, straining to hear every word. Arden Carson explained that he knew his Mary Francis was a handful to manage. If she needed a spanking, Daddy was to give it, same as he would his own girls. I knew that wouldn't be an issue, because Daddy didn't put up with bad manners or sassy mouths. Jackie and I both looked at each other, knowing that Mary Francis would have some tearful hours ahead 'til she learned to control herself better. Mr. C. was ever so grateful that Mary loved our family and felt so at home with us. He got a quivery voice when he thanked Mamma for the way she loved and cared for his little girl. He knew that she would get along just fine while he was gone, if we were there for her. Daddy and Mr.

Carson shook hands. Mr. Carson turned at the door to leave.

Daddy called after him, "Arden, you are not to worry about one single thing when it comes to that little girl of yours! I feel like she's half mine already. You just concentrate on getting well. Audrey and I will take care of Mary Francis. You have my word." The door shut quietly behind Mr. C, as Jackie and I scampered off to bed.

Keeping Mary close to our family in the days ahead seemed to make it all so much easier for Ruth Carson. She also had the added responsibility of looking after the store. Together, Mr. and Mrs. Carson had hired a new pharmacist to fill in while Mr. C. was away; that was a must, to keep the business going. Mr. Carson would do bookkeeping from the sanatorium, but Ruth Carson would have the weight of keeping the drugstore operational while he was recovering in the hospital.

Paul was to spend time with one of Mr. C's good friends, who had two sons for children. The oldest was slightly younger than Paul, but still old enough to be good company for him. Yet, when all was said and done, the Carsons were still their own family and wanted to be together as much as possible. Candice and James helped when they could. Medical school kept them both very busy; so, for Mrs. Carson that made for many long days and nights.

Throughout that difficult year while her daddy was away, Mary Francis spent the biggest share of her days eating at our table and keeping company with me and my sisters. When her mother was just too exhausted Mary spent the night, and sometimes several nights in a row. Mamma was found making supper for Mary and Paul right along with the rest of us on many days of that long and difficult year. Mary Francis liked it when we were together, 'cuz it made her forget how worried she was about her daddy. Mostly Mary didn't say out loud that she minded 'cuz her daddy was gone all the time, but she cried more often and fought with her mother frequently, even when Mrs. Carson did manage to get home from the drugstore at a decent hour.

Daddy, Mamma, and Mary Francis got along real well. After a few tough weeks, she learned to listen to Daddy the first time around. Usually she didn't have to be reminded more than once with Mamma. They worked that out real quick too. Neither did she have to have many spankings, which proved for happier days. In fact, she began minding in ways that she neglected to do with her own folks. Mary Francis learned to eat with her mouth closed, and not smack. She learned to talk less while her mouth was full of food. That behavior was not allowed at our table during any meal of the day. Mary was really trying to practice her manners. Mamma and Daddy watched for every chance to tell Mary how proud they were of the progress she was making toward becoming a proper Miss at the table. Mary Francis loved my parents and they loved her right back. We were the next best thing to real sisters.

The day Mr. Carson came back home from the sanatorium and was cured of the T.B. (remember, that's short for tuberculosis) was the happiest I had seen all the Carsons in a very long time. The whole neighborhood celebrated. The Carsons were ever so grateful for all the support they had gotten from everyone through the past year. Visits to the hospital, watching the kids, meals made and given, cards and flowers sent and enjoyed. Some of the dads took turns mowing the Carson's lawn when the family was away and Paul couldn't do it. Smiles were generously shared all around. We celebrated with a neighborhood potluck at the Carson's house so that Mr. C. could rest in his room if he got tired. Mrs. Carson arranged for the meat to be catered. The tables were filled with all the delicious food that everyone brought. The entire neighborhood welcomed Arden Francis Carson home.

Life returned to a more normal condition after a couple more weeks of recuperation and getting back into the routine that Mr. Carson had kept up before he got sick. After a few months it was as if he had never been gone, though he was home from work much earlier than before he had gotten sick with T.B. Mr. C. seemed grateful to be back at work. His smiles were more freely given. His easy, though infrequent, laugh was back. I loved that about him.

After a sleep over at Mary's house, I was always up before she was. So in the morning, it was not unusual for me to be at the breakfast table with Mr. Carson. I would sit with him picking at my Grape Nuts Cereal; a breakfast treat that I got only at their house because Mamma never bought it. He had taught me how to run hot tap water over the granules of dry cereal, let it set for a few minutes, then pour off the hot water, holding your hand or a table knife blade across the top of the bowl so that the cereal didn't spill out. Suddenly there you had it, a hot breakfast cereal, which still had a crunch when you ate it. Pour on a little milk and add the sugar. It was always remarkable to me how a warm bowl of anything could taste so good on a cold winter morning in Michigan, or any morning for that matter. Dad Carson would chuckle low in his throat as I sat there with my eyes shut savoring every bite of the breakfast in front of me. When I heard his gentle laugh my eyes opened wide. His long eyelashes made his eyes sparkle as he quietly said, "So glad you are enjoying your cereal, Miss Teresa Lee." He was a man of few words, but I always loved to hear him laugh, maybe because he did it so seldom. It was relaxing to be around him, because he always seemed so calm and slowed-down. Mr. Arden Carson had an easy way about him. We could sit at that table for long periods, sharing the view out the kitchen window, not saying a word, but feeling real comfortable just being there together. Sometimes I thought it was as though he was my dad, too.

Paul and Mary loved having their dad home again. They seemed to get along much better. Mary Francis was smiling more and resisting direction less. Paul was not picking at Mary every chance he got. Both were quieter and less demanding. That told volumes about how glad they were to be a family again. Life seemed to be humming along as it always did, but now even better. We were all grateful for that.

Chapter Thirteen

Party Lines

Mary Francis loved the telephone. She played with the phone on a daily basis. She loved pretending that she was a nurse receptionist at our local doctor's office. She gave directions over the phone as to what should be done about babies with fevers, dogs with toothaches, grandmas with cooking burns on fingers or worse, and brothers with serious black eyes and knots on the head from being whacked by baseballs, bats, or younger sisters. Of course, she always kept her finger on the disconnect button, at the bottom of the cradle where the phone's receiver sat, whenever she was doling out her advice. It was playing on the phone and that party line that got Mary Francis in a heap of BIG trouble, when she least expected it!

The old-style crank phones, which had previously hung on the wall, had cords only about 6inches long. You had to stand directly in front of the phone, hold the long cone-shaped receiver up to your ear and talk directly into the cup-shaped speaker on the front of the wall mount. If you were short, you had to stand on a stool to reach the phone. To make a call on the old phones, you had to crank the handle on the side for the number of rings you wanted. All of your neighbors answered to different numbers of rings. Newer wall phones had the style where the caller punched in the number buttons on the front face of the phone to get the number of the person you were calling. It was never a private conversation, and neighbors sometimes listened in on the conversations you were having with someone else. I guess that was how neighbors who lived in the country and in small towns kept up with the news, they just listened in on their friends' calls to other people or family members to find out what was going on with each kin group. Grandma always said, "You best not be saying things you don't want other people knowing or repeating, 'cause it sure won't stay quiet for long."

There was always a quiet click on the other end when someone, who wasn't part of the conversation, was listening. It was a dead give a-way, but also the lucky cue, to share only the things that you didn't care about others knowing. Some of the older neighbor ladies, who had nothing better to do, spent more time eavesdropping than others. Most of our moms were too busy to be spending time wasting an afternoon finding out something everybody else probably already knew. Sometimes people would just say, "Excuse us please, we are using the line right now, and we know you are listening." Then the usual "click" at the other end as their daily diet of gossip was suddenly squashed! Ah, party lines, the "Pot of Gold" for good gossip.

Newer models of phones now sat on tables, countertops, and desks, with longer coiled cords that stretched out a few feet from the phone. You could even walk a short distance away from where the phone was located in your house. Most people only had one phone in their residence. You could get them in four colors: black, white, beige, or gray. The new style phones had rotary dials, a round dial that you moved with your index finger. The ear pieces were longer now with rounded parts on each end that included a receiver that you listened from, and at the other end the speaker that you talked into. It was all in one piece that you held in the middle with your hand. The receiver sat in a cradle-like place at the top of the body of the phone, just above the rotary dial. Two rectangular bars would pop up when the receiver was removed from the cradle, which provided an open telephone line. The receiver sat in the bottom of the cradle so the call would disconnect as soon as you placed the receiver in the holder and the pressure of doing so disconnected the call. To dial the phone number you wanted, you stuck your finger inside one of the ten holes on the round clock-shaped dial. Printed within the ten circular finger holes were the numbers from one to ten, and the letters of the alphabet divided up between the ten holes. Phone numbers usually had six digits, sometimes letters substituted for numbers. The routine went like this: Insert finger into hole with the number or letter desired. Pull back the round dial to the silver stopper, let go when your finger hits the stopper. Select the next number/ letter with your finger and repeat the process, until the seven digit access is completed. Listen to the soft clickity sound of the dial as it made each turn. *I loved that sound.*

One of the first phone numbers Mamma taught me to dial was Grandma and Grandpa's phone number in Bancroft. I memorized that number like it was a song. I dialed Melrose 4-5226 (which translated 634-5226) and after one short and two long rings, I was talking to one of my beloved grandparents. How could a new and improved invention that made life so much easier at times, and was so much fun to use, get so many kids in hot water with their folks? The telephone was off limits to most kids I knew. Unless it was an emergency or permission was granted from parents to use the phone for a special reason, it wasn't to be touched. Those very rules of course made using the telephone all the more a temptation for anyone my age or younger.

Even with the newer model phones, one thing that had not changed for most people was the party line. Party lines were common ways that phone service was connected in small neighborhoods and country communities. That meant that other people knew when you were on the phone, because several families shared the same line. Private lines cost a lot more on your monthly phone bill, so most folks just kept up with the less private and less expensive party line. Doing that created some sticky problems, especially if you didn't want your neighbors knowing your business. It was common knowledge that people were prone to listening in on their neighbors' private conversations.

When kids, like Mary Francis, played with the phone, they best be sure that it was not connected. Misusing or playing with the telephone was trouble of a serious sort! If kids got caught playing with the phone, it wasn't usually even their parents that found them out. Often, it was a neighbor that snitched. Any foolishness, and the phone patrol was reporting, as soon as possible, violations to parents involved. Serious consequences were expected. That was the way it was when Mary Francis got caught.

Mrs. Waters lived on our street, right next door to my house. Before she had her house built there, we played games in the vacant lot. All the neighborhood kids were sad when that empty field became her spot on the block. Nevertheless, she came to share a party line with our side of the street. So did the Carson family. Mrs. Waters was older than both of my grand-mas. She rarely came out of her house, and when she did it was for short periods on very warm, sunny days. Her son visited once a week and shared dinner with her on Sundays.

Mrs. Waters liked a neat and tidy yard. She paid Dale Nelson one dollar and fifty cents a week just to mow her lawn, whether it needed it or not. She was friendly most all the time, except when you rode your bike on her lawn. At times like that, her front door would fly open and her face would look at you all pinchy-like and mean as she sternly commanded in the loudest voice she ever used, "Keep those bike wheels on the sidewalk and off my grass!" Same message every time, followed by her door slamming shut.

All the neighborhood kids concentrated real hard to ride a straight line down the middle of the sidewalk that ran past the Waters' residence. Or they might decide to take a route into the street past her stretch of the block, out of harm's way (relatively speaking of course). The neighborhood population under the age of twelve was mystified by the sweet conversations Mrs. Waters carried on with our mothers on those beautiful warm days when she felt like getting out of the house for a while. If they only knew!

We figured that she had to be watching constantly from her rocker in front of the picture window. She was like a spider on its web, just waiting for an unsuspecting victim to be preoccupied for an instant, which allowed their path to accidentally veer slightly off course and enter over enemy borders. She was suddenly up in a flash, yanking open her front door, forcefully sharing her memorized retort. Predictably we always got the same response consistently repeated by our mothers whenever we shared our protests of injustice...

"Now, now...Mrs. Waters is old and tired. She doesn't mean to be cross. She just likes a neat and tidy yard. Take extra care to stay off her lawn." So much for justice when you are not of voting age.

Mary Francis did not intentionally set out to get Mrs. Waters all riled-up by using the phone carelessly. However, she sure managed to do just that in a very dramatic way. But then, that was Mary Francis, always finding ways to create drama. Miss Mary got herself banned from the phone practically forever, and grounded for two whole miserable weeks. It all started so innocently. Who would have guessed? But knowing Mrs. Waters and her obvious strict attention to rules and borders, we should have known this would not turn out well for Miss Mary.

It all started with a snow day in Michigan. Just one day of the many unexpected holidays from school which comes from living in a state that can produce snow to your knees in a matter of only a few cold hours. The roads were completely plugged. School had been called off throughout the county. It was a wet, heavy snow. The kind of snow that is the hardest to shovel or move, ices-up fast, yet provides the very best conditions for making snowballs, snow forts, and igloos. All the neighborhood gang was outside in full force, as soon as some poor excuse for a breakfast was quickly consumed.

Everyone was ready to celebrate a day of no school, even moms and dads. The snow gear was on. Hats, mittens, coats, and boots were tied, buttoned, zipped, buckled, and snapped for a day of unrelenting abuse from snow and cold. The entire town was ready for sledding or skating down iced-over streets, sidewalks, and roads. All were ready to face surviving fierce snowball fights and truly enjoying the freedom that comes from an unexpected day off from school.

TERESA LEE

Mid-morning, after the cheers of "No School!" had long subsided and the chill of the day was setting in, Mamma called for us to come in for a warm-up with hot chocolate, which we welcomed with relief. Play pals who accepted the offer dumped boots, snow pants, hats, mittens, and gloves on the breezeway landing. Our outer clothes were sopping wet from the snow. We all piled into the kitchen sitting on the floor that ran around our salmon colored cupboards. Half the neighborhood under the age of twelve sat looking at each other over a steamy cup of hot cocoa. Mamma had added one large Stay-Puff Marshmallow to each mug for flavor and fun. Sets of crossed-eyes watched as the big fat marshmallow, floating on top of the hot chocolate, bobbing up and down, slowly melted down, getting smaller and smaller. It reminded us of our melting snowmen on warm sunny days. We laughed at the frothy marshmallow mustaches we all seemed to be wearing as we sipped away at the rich, yummy drink that warmed our tummies and toes.

As we sat trying out some new silly knock-knock jokes on each other, the telephone rang. Two short rings was our party line signal for a call to our house. Mamma quickly answered. It was Mrs. Carson inviting all of us to come over for some warm peanut butter cookies that she had just taken from the oven, her specialty, and a friendly game of Parcheesi. Both invitations held favorite choices which were hard to resist. Most of the boys lamented the loss of a warm cookie, but preferred the chance to play outside on one of the first snows of the coming winter. They argued that a game of Parcheesi could be played anytime. Mary Francis, Conrad, Bobby Starks, Jackie and I opted for warm cookies and a game, while the others were donning their winter gear once more and heading out for more snowy escapades. *When all was said and done, it would have been better if going back out into the snow had been our choice as well!*

Chapter Fourteen

Snow Day Dilemma

We arrived at Carson's front door in a matter of minutes with only snow boots and coats to get us quickly through the snow. A warm cozy spot, with fresh baked cookies and an inside board game to enjoy, was preferable to our pals' choice of braving the cold outside. Mrs. Carson greeted us at the door with a big smile and warm welcome. The smell of fresh baked peanut butter cookies hit our noses the instant we stepped inside. She laughed with us as we looked at ourselves in the big entry way mirror and mocked the funny "hat hair" we all were wearing. Mrs. C was home from work due to the Snow Day, too. Not for long though, since she had just gotten a call from one of the ladies who worked at the store. The store worker lived in the country, was snowed in and couldn't make it to work that day. Mrs. Carson would need to fill in at the drugstore.

We ate our cookies at the kitchen table over white napkins with blue snowflakes. *Nice touch on a snowy day*. We voiced our "Thank-yous" all around the table to Mrs. Carson and Mary Francis for the cookies and kind invitation. We got on with the business of playing a quick game of Parcheesi, while sitting on the warm carpeted living room floor. Bobby Starks and Jackie won the game as partners. Since only four players have spots on the Parcheesi board, someone had to play as a team. My sister and Bobby were the same age and in the same class at school, so they teamed up.

As a winner of the Parcheesi game, Bobby thought that he should get to choose the next game we played. He wanted everyone to go downstairs and play fire station, his favorite game. Bobby wanted to be a fireman when he grew up. Everyone in the neighborhood knew that Jeff Perrin's uncle was a fireman. Even better was the fact that Mike Frelund's dad was the fire chief in town. Bobby thought that was really neat! It didn't take long for us to get the basement set up like a fire station, since we had played this game many times before. Bobby was very particular about how everything should be. We used a play phone for the dispatch phone that came into the station with fire calls.

Mary's mother called down from upstairs, "Kids, I'm running to the store for an hour or so. Mrs. Payne is here to do some cleaning for me. Behave nicely and I will be back shortly. If you need anything, Mrs. Payne will help you."

Mrs. Payne lived only two blocks away. With all the snow, today she had walked to her weekly job of working for the Carsons, as their housekeeper, two days a week.

We answered in unison, "O.K. Thanks, Mrs. Carson. We'll play here in the basement."

"Bye, Mom. See you at dinner," Mary Francis chimed in.

We heard the back door open and close. Several minutes later the car could be heard backing out of the garage. The snow truck had gone past as we sat at the table earlier eating our warm peanut-butter cookies. A sure sign that the roads in our subdivision were now passable.

After we were satisfied that our "fire station" was ready and operational, Mary suggested that we have a fire run. Of course, Bobby jumped on that idea. He had appointed himself fire chief of course. A fire run was exactly the next best thing to do in his fire house. Mary Francis announced that since it was her idea first, and we were playing at her house, she would call in the emergency fire call. She added that she would go upstairs and use the telephone in the kitchen. After all, she reasoned, you can't be in the fire station when you make an emergency call! We all agreed that did make sense.

The plan was to leave the basement door open so we could hear the call. Using the phone in the kitchen wouldn't bother Mrs. Payne as she vacuumed the bedrooms in the back part of the house. We all agreed that using another phone was a good idea, that way our phone in the fire station would be freed up to take the call.

Conrad cautioned, "Mary Francis, do your parents let you use the phone for play?"

Mary quickly replied, "They don't care. Besides, I hold my finger down on the button so the call never really goes out. We are just pretending you know." As Mary Francis ran up the stairs with a pencil and paper pad in her hand, she called back over her shoulder, "Now don't pick up until you hear me say real loud: This is an emergency!"

Together we yelled back, "We got it!"

After a few minutes, the boys were growing impatient. "O.K., we are waiting!" Conrad hollered from the basement. "Remember to hold down the button!" he finished.

"Sh-h-h, we have to be quiet and listen for the call." Jackie shushed.

Still more minutes of waiting, then we heard Mary's voice, loud and clear above the running vacuum. We smiled at each other as she tried to disguise her voice.

"This is an emergency! My mother is away and our house is on fire! I live at the corner of Dartmouth Drive and Tuscola. My name is Conrad Douglas. Come quick!" Mary played.

"Why did she use my name? I didn't make the call! I'm one of the firemen! She doesn't even know how to play right." Conrad pouted with disgust.

Immediately those of us at the "fire station" began the sound of sirens with our voices as loud as we could while we scrambled around putting our fake fire gear on. Our "gear" turned out to be old rubber boots and some mildewed raincoats we had found in the Carson's Salvation Army donation box. Mary had found some of Paul's old plastic and metal play fireman hats in the blue wooden toy box behind the stairs. Getting all our "gear" on took a while longer than expected. Once we got to the part of putting on our fire hats, we wasted no time. Plopping them on our heads, we mounted the stairs to our "fire rigs" (the kitchen chairs lined up in rows).

We were loud as we scrambled up the stairs to rescue Mary Francis. So loud, that we couldn't hear the very real emergency going on just across the street from Carson's house. As we hit the top step, leading into Mary's kitchen, and the line of chairs that served as our fire truck, we all fell over each other at the sight of a very pale-faced Mary Francis. Hiding with her head ducked down, she was staring out the kitchen window. Suddenly a blare of sirens hit our ears. That sound was for sure **not** the siren sound that had been coming from our mouths. There was no mistaking the sound of a real siren!

"What's going on?" Conrad squeaked. "Why are all those fire trucks at my house?! Oh no, my house is on fire!" Conrad screamed as he bolted toward the front door, flapping his arms wildly.

"Oh dog poop!" Mary Francis whispered through clenched teeth. We all sucked in our breath at the use of her familiar expression for identifying real trouble. Instantly, we knew something was very wrong.

"Conrad, get back here! Your house is NOT on fire!" Mary hissed.

"What... What is happening?!" Conrad whined in total confusion. "Is this because you used my name on the phone? Why did you do that? You shouldn't have done that! You said it was pretend!" Conrad was totally losing it as he wailed out his complaints.

"Well, I couldn't use my name! The fire station is in my house. That would be just plain stupid!" Mary Francis seemed to be cracking under the strain. "We **were** playing after all!"

As we all stood peeking over the window ledge of the kitchen window, we could see fire trucks with lights and sirens blaring parked in front of Douglas's house across the street. Suddenly, the sweeper stopped. Mrs. Payne came running from the back of the house to find five scared children all standing in the kitchen with eyes glued to what was happening outside the window.

"What's going on? I heard sirens." Mrs. Payne asked urgently with a startled voice. Her eyes followed the line of stares focused on the excitement going on across the street.

"Looks like there might be trouble over at Conrad's house," Mary replied with a shaking voice. "I'm sure it must be a false alarm. I don't see any smoke," she continued with the innocent act.

Conrad started to protest, "It is all Mary Fr..." Mary's hand shot out to clamp tightly over his mouth and put a quick end to Conrad's response. We all stared at Mary Francis. Mrs. Payne stared at all of us.

At that point, the back door slammed open. My father, Mrs. Waters in her bedroom slippers, Mr. Douglas, Conrad's dad, and Mr. Joe Frelund, the **real** fire chief, were all standing in the doorway looking none too happy.

Without hesitation Mr. Frelund's voice boomed, "What's going on here?"

Mrs. Payne looked at all of us and squeaked, "Someone needs to start explaining!"

Mrs. Waters followed up with, "I knew it! She was disguising her voice, but it had to be Mary Francis, because the Douglas's are not on our party line! She's responsible!"

Due to being so unjustly accused (in her opinion) Mary Francis bolted past Mrs. Payne to the back of the house and into her bedroom, slamming the door so hard the whole house rattled. I could hear her shoving the beds against the door. This was a certain sign that the interrogation to come was not going to go well. Daddy walked to the kitchen phone, which was off the hook. He pushed the button down, waited for the dial tone and dialed the drugstore. Jackie and I looked at each other and immediately dissolved into a puddle of tears. Conrad and Bobby sat down hard on the top step of the basement stairs and put their heads in their hands without a word said.

Mr. Frelund talked quietly with Mrs. Waters as Dad talked to Mr. Carson over the phone. The fire chief encouraged Mrs. Waters to return home since there was obviously no fire, and the whole situation would be dealt with immediately. Mrs. Waters was thanked for her call to the fire department in preventing a possible tragedy had it been a real emergency.

She left with a very loud, breathy "Well, I never! Kids!"

Mrs. Waters shuffled down the sidewalk in very wet, snowy slippers and a too thin jacket. Mr. Frelund left without a word, walked across the street and ordered the fire trucks back to the fire station due to a false alarm. Momentarily Mr. Carson came screeching into his own driveway. Daddy, Mr. Douglas, and Mr. Frelund met him in the garage. They all talked quietly outside with Mrs. Payne and kept the backdoor shut tight.

Jackie and I, along with Conrad and Bobby, were now sitting on the floor of the kitchen in various locations looking at each other. We could hear Mary Francis banging the wall in her bedroom, probably rocking in her chair as she always did when she was upset. I was positively sure that she was crying, too. What had happened? Something had gone very wrong while she had been playing with the kitchen phone!

All of the adults re-entered the kitchen in single file with Mrs. Payne leading the way, head down and clearly unhappy. Daddy ordered the four of us to the kitchen table. Mr. Carson walked to the back of the house with stern purpose. You couldn't help but hear the forceful command he gave to his daughter from down the hall.

"Young Lady, you have thirty seconds to open this door or I'm coming in."

It wouldn't have been the first time that Daddy and Mr. C. had taken the hinges off the door to gain entry. With a degree of relief, we could hear the sudden sliding of the beds away from the door and the click as the lock opened. In less than an instant, Mr. Carson appeared leading Mary Francis by the arm. He led her silently to a seat at the same table already occupied by her four playmates, us. We all had red splotchy faces. We had all been crying, even the boys. *This was serious stuff!*

"All right, we want answers right now and the story better be right the first time it is told," Daddy ordered sternly.

"We are starting with you, Mary Francis", her father added with anger in his voice. Mary started to cry. "No tears until the story is told and we have the truth," he finished.

"A very serious situation was created this afternoon." The fire chief continued, "We need to understand exactly what happened here, so that it never happens again."

For the next hour these four fathers listened to the explanations that we all took turns providing. In the end, it was Mary Francis who took the brunt of the blame. She had after all been the one to make the call. Too bad she forgot about holding down the disconnect button on the phone. Even though it was an accident, it was still her fault. She hadn't even realized that her finger had slipped off the disconnect button because she was holding the phone in one hand and trying to write on her pad of paper with the other. While she was supposed to be keeping pressure on the disconnect button, she had been trying to design an award to present to the "Fire Chief", Bobby, for valiant service to a citizen in need... her. Mary Francis had gotten so distracted with getting that award designed just right, that she had forgotten about keeping the button down. Mrs. Waters had heard it all by accident.

Mrs. Waters just happened to be on the phone at the very same time talking to her sister, Alda. All Mrs. Waters and Alda heard was a young person saying earnestly that there was an emergency-- the house was on fire--and where the fire was-- then the line went dead. So naturally, Mrs. Waters immediately called the fire department, to sound the alarm. Well, she certainly did that part well! It became crystal clear that Mary Francis would be apologizing to Mrs. Waters and her sister, Alda, very soon. That was a popular consequence doled out for kids who ran amok. Make a sincere apology (in person) to those you have wronged. We hated doing it of course!

Days later, after talking the whole mess out, the whole gang agreed that we would all be better off without party lines, especially Mary Francis. We promised to share that with her in another two weeks when she wasn't grounded anymore. We never played with the phone again, and we sure didn't have to explain the why to Miss Mary Francis Carson. Within a month the Carson's had a private line. No more party lines for Mary Francis or her family, no matter how much a private line cost! Still, even with the new private line, she had to ask permission to use the phone for more than a year. *Ouch!*

Chapter Fifteen

Habitats

Friends come in all sizes and shapes, colors and personalities. I had skinny friends, chubby friends, and a friend with one good leg. I had a friend with a withered hand, and a friend who had been kissed by an angel. Joshua always carried that telltale streak of white hair in his otherwise dark brown bangs; a wisp of hair that would never be any other color. I had friends who enjoyed all different kinds of activities and games. I learned to enjoy friends with tempers and others with annoying habits who could always make me laugh. It's what's on the inside that counts.

I could see from the way the school day started that today was going to be great! Mrs. Parker, my second grade teacher, walked to the front of the class with her bright-eyed "We're starting something new" smile. She was using her famous Let's-Get-Excited voice and that always meant something special was in the works. Mrs. Parker loved to start new projects at school. She baited all of us with the lure early, which later in the morning, before lunch, became the hook used to get the new activity started with some degree of excitement. *What was this going to be about?*

The morning went by with an unusual amount of excitement in her step, which hinted the anticipation of something to come. Only fifteen minutes until lunch, and we were all sweating it out. We didn't like being dismissed late for lunch. *Why did she wait so long to begin? She knew how we hated being late for lunch. Could Mrs. Parker drop the awaited surprise, and get in everything she had to share regarding her special announcement in a quarter of an hour?* We hoped she'd be quick. We never saw her eat, so she probably didn't care about lunch.

Mrs. Parker began with what we had all been waiting to hear. Gushing with excitement, she announced, "This afternoon, we will get into our buddy groups and talk about habitats. I want to be sure that you have some time to think about this topic and talk to each other about the assignment." *O.K. good. She must be done. It's almost time for lunch. I was hoping that Mamma had not made my bologna sandwich for lunch too early so that it would sit out on the plate for too long. I hated warm bologna! Yuck!*

She continued to explain, "Habitats occur naturally in the world. People are greatly affected by the habitats they experience in their daily lives. People and animals in different parts of our world and country adapt in various ways to the habitat or habitats they face daily." She continued on with a determined expression that meant work ahead. "Habitats affect the way in which people learn to live and interact with their surroundings." *Maybe chips and chocolate milk when I get home.*

I knew this was my day! All of my second grade classmates sure could share a lot about habitats and I was secretly hoping that Charlie would be in my group. He was the expert about habitats in our class and in the neighborhood. Mary Francis and I had fun talking about Charlie's interesting habitat. Just this morning on our way to school, it was agreed that agreed we shouldn't be overly critical about his, since we both had one, too. I knew for sure that what Mrs. Parker said about habitats, affecting the way people live and get along in their surroundings, was the truth!

I wondered if Mrs. Parker was a mind reader. It was amazing that she would pick habitats for our discussion topic when (earlier before school started) we had just been talking about this very subject. Mrs. Parker hurried on to briefly explain something general about science and habitats; trying to get it in before the lunch bell. Most of her students were only half listening due to hunger.

Mrs. Parker was finishing up with what our assignment would be, "Decide what habitat each of you think would allow the greatest chance of survival. Give this some thought over lunch, talk to friends on the walk home. Later after returning from lunch, each group will talk about it some more. Also, be ready to share what good points and bad points can be discovered and listed about each kind of habitat?" Nineteen pairs of half-listening weary ears, and little staring eyes followed the ticking clock, as the eagerly anticipated ringing of the lunch bell finally sounded.

After a short talk on our way home for lunch, not one of us could figure out why Mrs. Parker thought habitats were so interesting to talk about in our buddy groups. It was a mystery to all of us why she even liked habitats and thought they were so important. Our parents didn't seem to like them one little bit. Mamma and Daddy were always trying to get me to stop my habitats. Besides watching me for any sign of returning to those persistent behaviors, sometimes Mamma was even after Mary Francis and Charlie to stop and leave the habitats alone! After my last not-so-good report card, Mamma and Daddy said that I was to try my hardest to listen and share my ideas when it was my turn. I sure had a lot of ideas about habitats, so I would try my best.

Besides Mary Francis, Charlie was my best boy buddy in the whole world. His real name, Charles Ivan Sinclair, Jr. was fancier than most, but everyone in the neighborhood just called him Charlie for short. Our dear teacher, Mrs. Parker, always called us by our proper birth names; "Because it taught us good manners", she said. Mrs. Parker would never call him anything but Charles. The kids on the block decided we liked "Charlie" best because it reminded us of one of our favorite T.V. chimps. You can never go wrong with a funny monkey! Besides, Charlie the Chimp was famous!

As we walked along, Charlie decided that his habitat was better than mine, but not nearly as interesting as Rudy Keller's or Judy Hickman's. However much it upset our parents or other people, was the measure we used to determine how good or bad each of us thought the other's habitat to be. I had to agree that Charlie's did cause quite a stir. Charlie got his habitat when he was four so he'd had his longer. I guess when you're more experienced about habitats you just naturally know more about the whole thing. Rudy bragged that he'd had his habitat since he turned two years old. I only got mine when I was five, and now we all were seven, so I was rather new in the area of long-standing habitats. Now finding the good part of a habitat was going to be the hard part. According to most of our parents, there wasn't one good thing about habitats. We were going to have to dig deep to find something good for Mrs. Parker's list.

TERESA LEE

On the way back to school from lunch, Charlie, Mary Francis, and I spied a sparkly rock in the sewer grate. We kicked the glittery rock down the sidewalk and talked over the new assignment that Mrs. Parker had just announced. We had decided that Rudy's habitat was worth watching closer. How in the world his mom ever thought that Rudy would want to share his habitat with the class, we just couldn't figure out.

Mrs. Keller, Rudy's mom, had come to school one morning the previous week real upset and was talking to Mrs. Parker for the longest time in the coat room; real quiet like, and all whispery, so we couldn't hear what was being said. We were supposed to be practicing our best manuscript. That means printing and staying in the lines, which no one liked to do anyway. So, listening was the first thing we all started doing. Rudy's face turned beet-red whenever his name could be heard in the whispered conversation. We couldn't hear everything but some kids heard this and some heard that and at recess we got together (Rudy, too) and put the story together like this.

Rudy liked his habitat and he even admitted that he did. His mom wanted him to wear his hat everyday with the hope that he would forget his habitat and leave it at home. Everyone knew it wasn't polite to wear hats in the classroom. But since Mrs. Keller was so upset and hopeful, Mrs. Parker told her they would try it for one week. Rudy said that he couldn't see how a hat was going to help him stop thinking about his habitat. We all agreed that moms and teachers have some pretty silly ideas. We figured that we would probably be upset too if our child's habitat was causing such big problems. After all you don't see many people seven years old losing their hair because of their habitat. Rudy agreed that having bald spots on your head at seven years of age wasn't a happy idea. Maybe wearing the hat would keep Rudy's habitat under control, but we didn't see how; since, he could just take his hat off anytime he wanted and his habitat would start taking over again. Rudy thought that maybe if some of us would just remind him whenever we caught him and say "Rudy, your habitat!" then he could get a handle on it and the hair would start growing back in again soon. Having the habit of twisting your hair out by the roots was no easy thing to give up on. Mostly he did it when he was bored or nervous, and it really got bad whenever he sat and watched the T.V. Westerns at night...especially if the bad guys were winning!

Mrs. Parker had just finished a week of lessons on the importance of individual differences and our part in being accepting and considerate of those things. We sure learned how to do that.

Just last Friday during math class Mary Francis calmly and considerately whispered to Judy Hickman," Blouse strings are not on the menu for lunch. Quit putting them in your mouth. If you keep sucking, chewing, and spitting on them, they will rot off and your mom will get mad at you! I'm just saying, since I would hate to see you get in trouble. Besides, having to look at spit covered shirt strings and dress collars is making me sick! I would really appreciate it if you didn't do that!" Judy just stared back at all of us with her big round doe eyes and kept chewing. *Yep, another habitat causing no end of trouble.* Could it be that studying habitats, according to Mrs. Parker, was her way of addressing problems and giving us practice in consideration?

How habitats fit in with science was a mystery to us. Rudy was sure to share all he knew about those. Charlie, Mary Francis, and I didn't want to miss a thing. We wanted to be in his group for sure so that we would get a good grade. Charlie and I had some

TERESA LEE

information on that subject ourselves, as our habitats were not small issues, especially to our moms. Oh my, could they get stirred up about habitats! I guess Mrs. Parker had no idea about those things yet, since she had no children of her own. We all figured that's why it was so easy for her to speak quietly and calmly about habitats. She just didn't know what it was like to live with a kid that had one!

Back at school that same afternoon, Mrs. Parker put us in groups of three boys and three girls. Rudy, Charlie, Mickey, Mary Francis, Katie, and I got to be together. We were elated since plenty of us in this group were masters at having habitats. We all agreed that Mary Francis had a great habitat that she could talk about. We didn't know about Katie or Mickey, but we'd sure be watching and listening. Of course, everyone in our group agreed Rudy should talk about his habitat first because his definitely was the most famous. After we got the full scoop on everything there was to know about the habit of twisting your hair until it came out by the roots, while watching T.V. or being too tired, we moved quickly to Charlie's.

Now Charlie's habitat was easy to figure out because we'd all seen it once or twice ourselves. It had suddenly appeared last year at the first grade Christmas program. Charlie was feeling dumb about being dressed like an elf. In addition, he was scared that he might forget his two lines. *"Hello, Santa! Where is Rudolph?"* As soon as we took the stage, and were standing in front of the smiling audience of family and friends, there it was...BLINK-BLINK-BLINK. His eyes kept blinking with a constant rhythm. His mother kept motioning for Charlie to stop his blinking. She would hold her own eyes wide open, stare straight ahead directly at Charlie, push her head forward like a gobbling turkey, and sit perfectly still. Much to her distress, no amount of reminding stopped it from continuing. The same habitat showed up again at the poetry recitation last spring when Charlie got up to recite, *"Three Little Dogs A-Wagging."* BLINK-BLINK-BLINK. The habit of blinking his eyes faster than any of us could count, was amazing! Rudy and Mary Francis had clocked him at forty-two blinks by the time his first poetry stanza was finished. Charlie was helpless to stop it.

Mr. and Mrs. Sinclair sure got mad about that blinking! As soon as all of us filed back to our classroom after the poetry performance, Charlie's dad grabbed him by the back of his coat and they were out the door in a flash! Charlie's eyes had stopped blinking as soon as his foot hit the bottom step of the stage stairs. So, by the time we got back to our schoolroom, he wasn't blinking at all. All the kids in our class wondered why Mr. Charles Sinclair, Sr. was still so upset! *Yep, parents could get riled up about bothersome habits.*

I guess all moms say the same kinds of stuff about habitats. No matter how different our habitats were; we all agreed-- we'd heard the same exact things. According to Mary Francis, she got the same old lecture every time she'd start in on her habitat, which was biting her fingernails. Her mom made her sit on her hands when her little daughter wouldn't stop. When it was really bad [her fingernails bitten a quarter of the way down her nail bed and bleeding] Mrs. Carson put Cayenne Pepper on the ends of Mary Francis' fingers so it would burn whenever she put her fingers in her mouth. Those circumstances proved to be no fun for either of them! Oh my no, then the tantrums began in earnest. Mary Francis learned to hide her habitat as often as possible after a few of those sessions, and her mother didn't push it.

TERESA LEE

We were sympathetic to each other when it came to consequences for letting our habitats get the upper hand. My habitat was chewing on my hair whenever I was tired or nervous during a T.V. show. Mamma threatened to cut my hair so short that I couldn't put my hair in my mouth because I wouldn't be able to reach it. I hated that threat. Two of my younger sisters had really long hair. They wore it in ponytails and sometimes braids that hung to the middle of their backs. Mine was shorter, but long enough to have a good chew on it whenever I needed comfort. Mamma would say how dirty my hair was and that I shouldn't be putting it in my mouth. I had a bath and my hair shampooed every single day, so I knew that wasn't the case.

It was the same routine; no matter which of us it was that was trying to live with a certain habitat. Bad habits didn't lend themselves to positive outcomes! Our parents threatened us if we didn't cut it out! The habitats we lived with certainly were not leading to easy paths for survival. Our parents seemed ready to crown us if we didn't stop our annoying habits and learn to control our actions. Why Mrs. Parker thought that habitats lent themselves to **enhancing** survival none of us had a clue! Maybe this unit of study was going to last a very long time. There certainly was a lot to be said about the subject, and with all of us being so experienced in the whole matter, who knew? It seemed a sure thing that Mrs. Parker was going to know more about habitats when this topic was over, than she ever thought possible. Like Grandma used to say, "You learn something new every day!"

Mrs. Parker surprised us all right! She acted as pleased as punch with our reporting out regarding the sharing in our buddy groups. After only two groups had shared what was said all around about habitats and views on the whole topic, she sat at her desk and laughed until the tears ran down her face. The entire class sat silently, paralyzed with fear, as we witnessed the complete break-down of our dear teacher. She couldn't even catch her breath as she tried to explain why she was gasping for air between uncontrolled bouts of laughter. We nodded heads all around, agreeing with certainty that everyone would surely get a good grade on this science unit. Our teacher seemed absolutely filled with joyfulness as she laughed and giggled her way through our reports. I guessed that we had the right idea and the rest would be a cinch.

After a while, Mrs. Parker gained control of her fits of laughter. She went on to explain that a very serious misunderstanding had occurred. She added, "Tomorrow we will be starting over again with a new and different approach to habitats. I have appreciated all the obvious thought you exerted in sharing your ideas and trials with years of work on either breaking or perfecting your very own habitats. I will share, more clearly with you tomorrow, my ideas about **habitats**. In addition, we will be watching a filmstrip about the African Rainforest."

Every second grade student was silent, including me and Mary Francis. We all were wearing the same confused looks on our faces. Each wondering in their own head: *Whatever in the world did an African Rainforest have to do with habitats? This was a subject so easy to explain, and with no 8 millimeter filmstrip necessary.*

Chapter Sixteen

Going West

Over time, you realize that a special pal will be one of your most treasured friends forever. Why? It's plain. You always find a way to fix the friendship when it breaks. Sometimes you can be so mad at your best friend that you think you will never look their way or speak to them again, but it doesn't last. You just can't help yourself. Together you glue the cracks and cement the friendship. Best friends always find a way back to each other, because there is no one else quite like them. For you, your best friend is "One in a Million."

It sure wasn't any idea of mine to take up moving out West. I didn't like the notion one bit, and you can be sure Mary Francis wasn't buying that idea either. You can imagine what sort of things she had to say about the whole mess! It was fearsome even thinking about moving. How could we leave behind Grandpas and Grandmas that we had spent half of our life with, every week and mostly every day, since we'd been born? It was unthinkable, and would prove to be the hardest thing we'd yet to do in our young lives. Having to pick up with a new group of friends, just when we were getting on so well with ours, was purely exhausting just trying to imagine it all. No Sir-eee moving was not for me... or Mary Francis!

Daddy blamed a good buddy of his, Mr. Norman Hatcher, for planting that little seed of an idea in his head about moving West to New Mexico. Daddy had known him from when they had served together in the Navy during World War II, on the *U.S.S. Tennessee.* Norman lived with his family in Texas and was making a great wage in the construction business. The idea had laid quiet in Daddy's mind for a long spell. He wasn't even sure just when it had started sprouting into a regular full grown, giant-sized idea. In any case, the fruit of it ended in giving Daddy the itch to move. Personally, I considered it one bad seed! The very idea of us moving was dreadful! Mary Francis cried for days and I did, too.

Getting work had slowed down considerably. Money was tight for a lot of people in Michigan in 1958, and new house building had come to a virtual stand-still. All the grown-ups called it a recession. Daddy's friend, Mr. Hatcher, told him about this new and growing company in Albuquerque, New Mexico. The business was booming, growing so fast they couldn't keep up with the orders. Daddy was sure that building kitchen cabinets precut and in an assembly line was the reason they were producing huge amounts of product every day. People living in the West were still in the midst of a building boom. People were moving to the warmer climates with work easier to find. Daddy thought it would be a good venture and work was guaranteed. My dad wasn't afraid to try anything. Just like in the nursery rhyme, *"Mary Had A Little Lamb"*, where my dad went my mother was sure to follow and so were

TERESA LEE

his four little girls. That was a given. Mary Francis and I begged my parents to reconsider.

After a number of busy months at working to find a suitable buyer for our first real home, to which we were all fondly attached, the house sold. We would finish out the school year, me in fourth grade, Jackie in third, and Christie in first grade. Cathy wasn't in school yet. She was still only four. Mamma would have no part of moving in the middle of the school year. Daddy would have to be content staying put so as to finish out the school year. She argued, "Maybe by then, the girls will be more settled with the whole moving idea." Really, did we have a choice? When Daddy made up his mind, there was no going back. I was very sad, somewhat mad, and already homesick. Mary Francis was just plain mad!

Saying goodbye to all of our neighborhood friends was painful enough, but having to leave Mary Francis behind was just too hard to bear. Leading up to the days just before we were to leave, she had been overly irritable even for Mary Francis. Her mother was worried about the effect it was having on Mary, and although our mothers promised that the two of us could talk on the phone every week, it wasn't enough to keep her even partially satisfied.

Mary Francis took to crying and throwing tantrums. She stomped out of the house screaming, "NO, NO, NO!!" when she saw the first of the packing boxes lining our kitchen walls. She wouldn't come back in the house for three days.

One especially bad day, because the time for us to be moving was getting closer, Mary Francis raged the best part of one whole afternoon, "I'm never speaking to your dad ever-ever again! I hope all the tires go flat on his stupid trailer, too! I'm not even going to say good-bye to him! I will to everyone else, but not to him!" I tried to reason with her and remind her about the good times we would have when we got together at holiday time. It was useless. Nothing worked.

She stomped home screaming, "I hate him for moving!" I knew she didn't really mean it, but it still made me cry. She loved Daddy about as much as anyone in my family. Daddy understood her almost as well as me. She was really hurting and so were both families watching what she was going through. On one of those really hard days, Mary Francis barricaded herself in her bedroom and stubbornly declared, "I'm not coming out until Mr. Cole swears on the Bible not to move!" She had shoved every piece of furniture that she could possibly move in front of her bedroom door. She was not about to budge. She had been in her room for most of the day and missed her lunch and supper. I had tried to reason with her through the screened window, but no use. She was in no mood to listen to anything about moving!

Daddy and Mr. Carson had to take her bedroom window out and push me through the skinny window opening to unlock the door and help get the furniture out of the way. All the while I was trying to talk some sense into my best friend. Suddenly she just threw herself down on her bed and sobbed like she would never stop. I laid down beside my best friend in the world, put my arm over her back and waited with tears running down my own cheeks, until she cried herself to sleep.

It took some time, but she finally decided that all of her screaming, crying, and tantrum throwing wasn't going to change Daddy's mind. She was so right. After that, we both resigned ourselves to it and tried to enjoy every minute of the time we had left. Daddy had promised we would come home for Christmas and that made it a little more tolerable. Daddy never broke his promises. Mary Francis and I had already planned our Christmas-**week** pajama party.

For two months, Daddy and Grandpa had been busy building a trailer that would carry all of our belongings across the long trek that was to haul us hundreds of miles away from home and all the people we loved so well. Daddy had bold letters painted on the side of the trailer to advertise his trade so that when we got to New Mexico he would get extra work. It said:

Derwood C. Cole
Building Contractor and Cabinet Maker
Quality Workmanship.

A space was left to add our new phone number when we knew what it was to be. After all, it was going to take a bunch of money to move and set up house in a brand new place, so it was a sure thing that Dad would be 'moonlighting' as Grandpa liked to say. That meant working long hours after his regular job was done at the cabinet factory doing odd jobs for pay.

The trailer was covered with shiny silver tin. It was no bigger than a hay wagon with tall sides and a shoe-box top. "Good and water tight," Daddy said. Grandma and Mamma packed up that trailer to the tippy-top with stuff needed for setting up our new house. Everything was wedged in from side to side, with little space to spare. Only a narrow strip, just inside the double doors at the back, was saved for serving up the picnic lunches we would be eating on the road. It also provided space for packing in the groceries we'd be buying along the way in cities and towns we traveled through. Mamma and Grandma had made special red and white checked curtains. They fit the station wagon windows just right and would keep the sun from heating the inside of the car too much, as we traveled west. All preparations seemed in place and the final days of living in the neighborhood were drawing to a close.

Friends in our neighborhood held a big going away party several days before we left. Tearful goodbyes and promises of "We'll get together at Christmas, when you're home" were said. Before our leaving, hands were shaken in earnest all around, for good-luck and good health to each, until we all met again. All the kids from the neighborhood, along with their parents, couldn't keep the tears from flowing that day. We were like family. Leaving and losing love that has filled your life is never easy.

The last day in the neighborhood dawned a day like any other, but it **wasn't** a day like any other. It was a day never to be forgotten. Worst of all? The final hugs from the Carsons. As Mary Francis stood with tears streaming down her face and her bottom lip quivering uncontrollably, it was too hard to bear. Even Paul had tears in his eyes that day, as he hugged my dad hard around the waist, and Daddy hugged him back. After all her protesting, Mary Francis even had hugs and kisses for Daddy. He scooped her up and squeezed her tight for a long time. As he put her down, with his usual tickle under the chin which she always expected, her usual giggle in response to the tickle was missing. This day it was replaced with salty tears and a very weak smile. We took pictures of tear stained faces and forced smiles. At last the final "goodbyes" were done. Mary Francis stood in her yard with her mother holding tight to her hand. Mary was jumping up and down and screaming, "Please, Mr. Cole don't leave!! Please!!" But there was nothing to be done about it. The going had been decided long before.

Daddy drove the car away with the faces of four little girls pressed tight against the windows of our 1957 black Ford station wagon. Mamma was crying, too. She sat with her back as straight as a board, staring directly out the front windshield of the car. Mamma hoped that we wouldn't know, but we did. Through our own tears, Jackie and I could see the tears streaming down her cheek and dripping off her chin. She dabbed at her eyes with her hankie, but never made a sound. Those red and white checked curtains, hand sewn with such care, were tear stained and wet from the crying that took place over the next twenty minutes as four little girls said their final good-byes in the only way that was left.

We drove to Grandpa and Grandma Jackson's house for an overnight stay before we were to take off on this new and overwhelming adventure the next morning. Grandma dried our tears and surprised us with a special cake that she had made for us to take on our trip. We would be eating it along the way, and remembering how much she loved us with every bite. We ate all our favorite foods for supper that night: Hamburgers Deluxe, with all the trimmings, homemade potato salad with pickled beets, and lots of chips, homemade ice cream for dessert with Grandma's chocolate chip cookies, the best in the whole world. Grandpa and Grandma Cole joined us for our farewell picnic in the backyard. It would be the last picnic we would have together as a family for a long time.

The next morning dawned clear and sunny. "Bright and early," was Daddy's designated time for departure. It was a day none of us would ever forget. It was the first time I ever recalled seeing my daddy and grandfather cry. Grandma was hugging Mamma like it was the last time she'd ever be seeing her. Both were trying to hold back the tears. Mamma was trying real hard to be brave and not cry so as not to upset the Little Girls too much. But, we already were and had been for days, so all of Grandma's and Mamma's efforts were really for nothing. It was when Grandpa took Daddy's hand in a real tight loving handshake and looked straight into his eyes, that I could see the tears glisten in my Daddy's eyes, too. Grandpa was not afraid for anyone to see the tears coursing down his face. Quick as a wink, Grandpa gave Daddy the biggest hug that he'd probably had since he was just a boy. The two men who my sisters and I loved most in the whole world, both stood there holding on to each other tight, with their tears washing each other's cheeks. It was one of the saddest days of my young life and even though I was biting my lip trying to be brave, being the oldest and all, I was certain my heart was as heavy and hurtful as I'd ever remembered it being for the ten short years I had lived.

Saying goodbye to Mary Francis and the neighborhood gang was hard enough. It included the using up of a whole brand new box of Kleenex tissues. Several of us sported red puffy eyes for one whole day and a better part of the next. I felt real lonesome about leaving and strange, like it was all part of a dream and not really happening. However, this deep hurt of having to say goodbye to my grandparents, was something entirely different. *It was like a part of me was being left behind, like I'd lost an arm or leg or some part inside of me that I couldn't see. It was nearly making me sick to my stomach, the way my heart would start hammering and thumping when I thought of not seeing Grandpa and Grandma for who knew how long? It was a feeling born of misery.*

The first few hours of riding in the car were real quiet except for the crying. Everybody would just get settled down and it seemed that the worst of the tears was

TERESA LEE

over. Then all of a sudden, the sniffling could be heard yet again. It started real soft, smothered in a hankie. It took only seconds to be increased again into a good cry, passing from one to the other. It seemed contagious like a yawn. Mamma had gone through about five handkerchiefs handing them from one to the other of her sad little girls. She even used one herself as she passed it along. Every single one sopping wet!

Finally about lunch time, I guess my dad had figured enough was enough, and we had better pull ourselves up by our boot-straps, get on with life and begin moving forward. He pulled the car over on the shoulder of the road turning around to face us.

Daddy spoke with authority in his voice, "O.K. enough of this crying! It isn't like someone died or something!"

I thought to myself: *It couldn't feel much worse than this if someone did!*

Daddy continued more gently, "We are together, and everything is going to be just fine. I am absolutely keeping my promise about Christmas back home in Michigan this year! So, no more tears, including Mom here. We are off on our adventure together. We are going to see some very interesting things! Now, where shall we have lunch?" He finished with an enthusiastic question.

He faced front again, and pulled the car back onto the road. Dad drove on while everyone rode quietly with no sniffles or tears for several miles. No one answered his question. *Who feels like eating anyway?* My mind sassed back at him in secret.

After only a few more miles of driving, he suddenly turned the car, with the attached trailer, into a drive-in A & W Root Beer Stand located in a town we were passing through. Steering the car to a stop, Daddy turned with a smile and announced, "Anyone seen or heard crying, in the time it takes to put our order in, won't be deserving of a fluffy, foamy root beer served in an ice chilled mug."

Well, I can tell you that put an end to the crying, leastways for the time being.

After we all had slurped up the last drop of root beer clinging to the sides of those ice-cold mugs with the orange and brown A&W printed on each side, we were back on the road again. Mamma soon suggested that we should all sing *"You are my Sunshine."* It was one of Grandma's and Grandpa's favorite songs that we all sang together. Mamma also reminded us that they were probably singing it themselves, as they were sitting down to their dinner, smiling big and knowing that we were singing it, too. *I don't think so! Grandma is still crying just like we are and she will be for days!* Even at ten years, I knew that my Grandma and Grandpa were the saddest of all.

Anyone passing by our 1957 Black Ford station wagon adorned with pretty red and white checked curtains at the side and back windows and pulling a very new shiny trailer, would never have guessed the heavy hearts it carried. Our strained rendition of that favorite country tune drifted along with us, sung bravely though not loudly. No one passing by would ever know the life changing events being covered over by a favorite song that flowed from the open windows of a most peculiar little caravan travelling west.

Miles of driving and hours of trying to find something to do to pass the time was trying for all of us. Grandma and Mamma had filled a box full of games, crayons, pencils, paper, and books that were to help with the boredom of such a long trip. We managed well most of the time, but sometimes there was nothing that seemed to help. No amount of coaxing could distract Cathy or Christie when they were tired. The tears flowed with no let up, because all they wanted

TERESA LEE

was their own bed and to be home in our little house. Sometimes a stop was just what was needed.

One afternoon of our travels, Mamma mentioned to Daddy that we were running low on lunch supplies. Cathy had been crying for almost twenty minutes. It was clear, that a break from the car was needed. Every day since we had crossed the state line of Michigan, the cooler in the back of the trailer that held our sandwiches, drinks, and other food items needed frequent refills of ice; another good reason for stopping. We had only just crossed the southwest corner of the Kansas state line the night before. For most of the morning, we had driven through the southwestern pan-handle of Oklahoma. We were traveling along a state road that would carry us into New Mexico. It was way past lunchtime by the time Daddy made the stop that Mamma requested. We were in a town located in the northwest corner of the Texas panhandle. *Who knew what town? By now it all blurred together.*

Daddy parked in front of a small grocery store that lined the main street. Everyone got out of the car and stretched some very cramped legs for several minutes. We enjoyed just standing for a while. Cathy was smiling once again. We all had a drink of water before we went in to shop for the things Mamma had on her grocery list. We walked into an air-conditioned grocery store with wood-planked floors and a jingle bell on the door. *Just like the stores at home.* We had been in the car for a good share of the morning without a break. We all needed a bathroom stop and **pronto**, before any of us could concentrate on the items we needed to get.

We had started toward the back of the store, walking in the direction the lady at the cash register had pointed out to us, as soon as we crossed the threshold. I guess she knew exactly what was needed when my mother walked in with four little kids on her heels, like a mother duck with her ducklings; that could only mean one thing. Suddenly, all of the 'ducklings' following in a line, plowed directly into Mamma's back at her abrupt halt. She put her arms out to block our advance and stood very still looking at a sign posted directly over the drinking fountain, located between the two doors marked Men and Women. Even my six year old sister, Christie, could read that sign. She read aloud the words my mother stared at but could not speak: WHITES ONLY. NO COLOREDS ALLOWED.

The usual pink hue had completely drained from Mamma's face, as she continued to drill that sign with her eyes. Without the slightest hesitation, she turned instantly on her heel, grabbed each of my two youngest sisters by the hand, and bumped right into Daddy, who was himself heading to the back of the store for the same purpose as the rest of us.

"What's going on?" Daddy questioned Mamma with surprise. She brushed past him marching toward the entrance, clearly upset. Jackie, Daddy and I stood together wondering what in the world she was doing. On her march away from us she proclaimed with anger,

"We are **not** spending one **single** dime of our money in any store having a sign **like that** on the premises!"

"What sign?" Daddy asked clearly perplexed as he had not reached the back of the store as we had, so had not seen the sign posted there on the wall. I took Daddy's hand and turned to point at the sign causing Mamma so much distress.

Christie still being pulled along by my mother looked back at my dad and pleaded, "Daddy what does whites only mean? Mamma didn't like the sign! I have to go potty!"

"You bet I didn't!" Mamma snapped over her shoulder looking directly at the check-out lady.

TERESA LEE

Daddy did a quick turn around and walked out of the store on my mother's heels without answering my little sister's question. He never looked at the woman still standing behind the counter. That meant that Daddy wasn't happy about that sign either.

Mamma stomped to the car. We all piled into the back seat once more, and began looking wide-eyed at each other. Without a word, Daddy started up the car and drove off.

My two youngest sisters recovered from their surprise at the sudden turn of events and tearfully started in,

"Mommy, I hungry. I hungry now! Cathy began her familiar littlest sister whine.

"Daddy, I have to go potty so bad!" Christie pouted.

"Mamma, what does whites only mean?" Christie persisted in her unanswered plea. "Daddy, why did that make Mommy so mad?" She kept on when my mother gave no answer either.

Mamma only mumbled disgustedly, "Well, I never! The very idea of such a thing!" She continued staring out the front windshield fuming.

"Let's go to the gas station and ask where the next closest grocery store is," Daddy suggested. "These girls are hungry and need a bathroom break." Daddy finished, trying to reason with Mamma.

"Well you just go ahead and do that, but I'm not setting foot inside any place that has a sign like that and that is final!" Mamma growled.

Thank goodness, no sign like that was in the gas station where Daddy stopped. We all used the restrooms and that seemed to settle Mamma down a bit. Daddy got directions to another grocery store down the road a few miles. We all went in, and again no signs like the ones in that first store were anywhere to be seen. We got everything on our list of groceries, with ice for the cooler. Daddy paid our bill, and found a nice park in the town with a picnic table where we could sit and relax outside the car. Mamma put a quick lunch together from the items we had purchased. As usual, we said our mealtime prayers. None of us took one bite, but waited for what we knew was coming next. Then, Daddy explained the sign.

Only Jackie and I really understood the sad and unfair meaning held in Daddy's words of explanation. Little Cathy had no idea what any of his words meant, being only four. Christie was confused thinking it had something to do with taking crayons into the bathroom. She couldn't get the idea that it all had to do with the color of people, not crayons. Mamma finished the entire conversation by stating very firmly, "We will not be talking of this any further. Anyone who would hang a sign like that, in plain sight of any person, is not fittin' to have their business in the first place! That's not our way and every single human being deserves the same regard as the next! I don't care if they're purple!! Now, everyone EAT!" Clearly, Mamma was still riled up!

" Well said, Mrs. Cole! I'm starved! How about everybody else sittin' around this table? Let's dig in!" Daddy ended as he and Mamma passed around the paper plates piled with sandwiches, chips and one dill pickle each for good measure.

During the rest of our time getting there and living out west, we did see signs like the one in the grocery store every now and then. It was always the same reaction by both my parents. We wouldn't do business in any place that had signs like that, and with good reason. My sisters and I never fussed about having to leave to find a different place, even when once it happened to be at an ice cream parlor. My sisters and I came to know very well what those awful signs meant.

TERESA LEE

One man's words stuck in my head as we marched out of his store which was hung with those kinds of signs. "Oh, y'all Northern Yankees! You's all the same! See if I care if I get y'r business or not! He snarled. "Just git back where you came from!" Mamma and Daddy didn't pay him one second of attention, walking out with heads held high. They didn't care one whit about him, his business, or his hateful thoughts and words.

*I sure know I'm **not** home and I'm real proud that I am a 'Northern Yankee'!*

Chapter Seventeen

Making the Best of It

The heat was the thing. Every single morning since our little caravan had rolled into Albuquerque, New Mexico it had been the same. That blazing sun poking his eye up over the edge of daybreak, peering strong and steady without a blink, emitting the reddest glare you could imagine. So began yet another scorching day in the Southwest. Another day of counting the length of time that we had been away from our home in Michigan and the family and friends we loved so well. Another day of getting through the sweat that came just by sitting still. Another day of feeling that dusty cough in your throat that never eased up until you were drinking a long, tall glass of cool water. It was a daily routine consuming minutes of every hour that the sun was full up in the sky.

Every day was exactly like the day before. No matter how long we looked up, never did we see a floating wisp of cloud to hide the sun for one instant. No welcomed relief from the oppressive and relentless assault of heat. Each morning, that Old Sun would just keep rising up through the azure blue sky over New Mexico. Its piercing rays burning a rainbow path of orange, yellow and white 'til the smoldering spark of it would suddenly explode in full flaming heat. That southwest sun could bake, as dry as clay, any living thing existing beneath it, which didn't have the good sense to take a portion of shelter from its persistent radiance. No matter how dry of a heat it was, **it was hot**!

Daddy and Mamma were lucky to find and rent a two bedroom house trailer, just like new, double wide, in a mobile home park at the edge of Albuquerque, New Mexico; the largest city of the state, and about two hundred-seventy miles from the United States border into Mexico. We stayed there while they looked for a suitable house for us to live. The bedrooms were small, but the living space at the other end had enough room for everyone to sit comfortably. It doubled for the dining area where we ate, with a table on a pole in front of the couch. Our bedrooms were in the back, at the far end of the trailer. Mamma and Daddy slept in one room, and my three sisters and I slept in the other room. The two bunk-beds created the space for sleep-ing, with two little girls in each bed. It was smaller than we were used to, but we were managing.

Mamma was up early every morning, sent Daddy off to work, and then hurried about getting her hard work done before the heat of the day got too much of a start. It had taken her the good part of a week after we moved in, to get that trailer scrubbed as clean as a whistle. At last, she was more satisfied with how it looked. Just as Mamma liked, it sparkled with clean windows, shiny floors, and polished countertops.

A weekly routine was two trips to the Laundromat just around the corner. Mamma didn't like that at all. She especially didn't like the way people stared at us as we walked one block down to do the wash. She always made us walk close to her and hold on to her skirt or the laundry basket. This neighborhood wasn't used to seeing blonde-haired, blue-eyed neighbors. Most of our neighbors, as far as I could tell, had straight black hair and dark suntans. They also weren't used to seeing curly hair, polished fingernails, and red lipstick, which Mamma had always worn every day. Weary lines always showed on her face at the end of a day after we had done the laundry. We just didn't fit in here.

Most of our new neighbors were from Mexico. They were people who went about their business quietly and pretty much left us to ourselves. Since we were new to the park, Daddy thought that they really didn't trust us yet. After all, **we** were the strangers. They were always talking in Spanish to each other, so most of the time we had no idea what they were saying. I thought they liked it that way. Most of our neighbors could speak English, but the older ones just not so well. You had to listen carefully and fill in the blanks of broken English they skipped over. I wondered too, what they were saying to each other in Spanish while we were standing right in front of them. We had no idea if the conversation of chatter between them was about us, or if what they were saying was nice or not. Mamma always just flashed her friendliest smile and walked on to wherever we were going.

Those first weeks in Albuquerque were some of the longest days I knew. I was also quite sure they were some of the most miserable days Mamma could ever remember. She missed Grandma something awful. Tears instantly welled up in her eyes whenever one of my little sisters started crying for Grandma and Grandpa, pleading to go home. Both were too young to understand that our home was wherever Mamma and Daddy happened to be. Daddy always seemed to know when we had an especially bad day. After supper dishes were cleaned up, he would surprise us all with a trip to the ice cream shop three blocks down the street.

That invitation immediately brought smiles back and all was forgotten at least for the rest of **that** day.

Besides the heat and the dust, we had to be patient with how sad Mamma was most of the time. She was real homesick for Michigan, and so were we. Like everything else here, we had to wait patiently for a phone to be installed in our trailer. We finally got one during the second week there. Now we didn't have to use the pay-phone at the entrance to the trailer park anymore. Mamma cried whenever she got a letter from Grandma. Her sadness usually made my younger sisters start crying. It was worse if Mamma **talked** to Grandma and Grandpa on the phone. We had to save our extra money for the pay phone calls to our Grandmas and Grandpas that Mamma and Daddy made at least once a week. Other calls had to wait awhile.

At last, Daddy could make good on the promise made for Mary Francis and me to talk every week. Mr. and Mrs. Carson even sent Daddy money to pay for the calls and never complained about how long we talked. Mamma had kept it to herself that Mary Francis had been sick for weeks after we had moved. She was even in the hospital for three days because she got so distraught and worked up over us leaving. Mamma never told me until a long time later about how hard it had been for Mary Francis. Mamma knew that I would be very upset. Mrs. Carson told Mamma that the calls were important to Mary Francis for her well-being. Even Mr. Carson, who was known to watch the way he spent his money, didn't care how much the calls cost. He was paying for them because his Mary Francis was ever so much happier after we had talked on the phone. Those calls meant the world to both of us.

In order to show good manners and not take advantage of this generous offer, Mamma insisted we keep our calls to no more than 15 minutes. We both looked forward to that weekly call more than anything! Every now and then we even got to talk twice in one week, especially if Mary was having a bad day. Mary Francis spent the better part of our phone calls satisfying my appetite for news of the gang. I loved every minute spent filling me in on details and stories, catching up on what was happening with everyone and reporting about how our forts were holding up. I told her all about the long trip to New Mexico, and some of the wonderful things we had seen. I also told her about the nasty sign in the grocery store and others seen along the way. She fumed about how much it had upset Mamma and Daddy each time.

"What's the matter with some of those people out there?" she questioned with irritation. "Why are they so nasty? Good thing Abe Lincoln isn't still around, they would be in big trouble! I'd say they sure need some prayin' for at church!" *Yep, my best friend, always seeing eye-to-eye with me on the most important things. Gee-whiz but I miss the old neighborhood!*

I got a call from Mary Francis about once a week, and every week more tears spilled after the phone was hung up. I missed Mary Francis something fierce. I kept a picture of the two of us taped to the wall by the bed where I slept. I knew she was missing me, too. I bet her eyes stung with tears like mine did, most nights before they closed in sleep. My head just couldn't turn off the pictures of us running in the park or riding our bikes, always together. Other nights before my eyes closed in sleep, I could see Grandpa and Grandma in the kitchen at their house, sitting and staring at each other, not knowing what to do with us all gone. The tears would come again and wash my eyes until they were too blurry to see, and I finally surrendered to slumber. *"There's no place like home!"* Now I know *what Dorothy, in the* **Wizard of Oz***, meant when she said that.*

I missed the dreamy refrain of the trains that I used to hear from my bed at home. That familiar sound had been replaced by the not so familiar sharp-edged blare of police car sirens and ambulance screams that come with living on the edge of a big city. More often than we liked, after nearby sirens brought us abruptly out of our sleep and filled us with uneasy feelings, we'd hear the pounding sound of running feet. Sometimes more than one set, racing close-by through neighboring trailer lots or down the graveled road that wound through the park. Daddy always got up for a while after times like that and sat silently on the front room couch in the dark. I never knew exactly why he did that. I guessed it was because he couldn't get back to sleep.

Our family never knew what to expect each morning when we swung that trailer door open to walk out into the morning air. Maybe little horned lizards would be sunning themselves on our cement slab at the bottom of our trailer steps. Once in a while, a neighbor's lazy cat would be laying on the bottom trailer step sleeping in the morning sun. One particular day when Daddy opened that door, about to leave for work, he was met with a surprise none of us would ever forget!

It was Wednesday morning, the third week of living in the trailer park. Jackie and I were up in time to share a glass of juice with Daddy as he finished breakfast and was almost ready to leave for work. My two littlest sisters were still asleep. He had opened the always locked inside door about half way as he started to leave for work. With his lunch pail in one hand, and his other hand still on the door knob, Daddy hesitated a moment to turn back and give my mother a final kiss good-bye. He raised his hand for a good-bye wave to Jackie and me as we sat watching from the couch. As

TERESA LEE

he turned to step out the doors, he suddenly stopped dead in his tracks, hearing the rattle of the snake begin!

The heavy inside trailer door was swung fully open against the inside wall of our trailer. Just beyond, was the partially opened outside screened door. As Daddy looked down to discover the unfamiliar rattling sound, he found himself face to face with a very big, Diamond-Back rattlesnake. It had coiled up on the middle step of the trailer stairs, soaking up the first rays of morning light. The snake raised its head at the movement, and Daddy slammed that screened door shut so fast and hard, the whole trailer shook from the force. That SLAM brought Jackie and me and our still sleepy brains to full attention in an instant. We both jumped from the couch and started toward our clearly startled parents. Mamma was standing directly behind Daddy so she had heard the rattle of the snake as well. Jackie and I knew something was wrong, but had not heard the sound due to our spots on the couch and its distance from the door. Mamma held tight to Daddy's shirt, peering around from the side, as he slowly opened the door again. We all stared through the screen into the beady eyes of a snake bigger than I had ever seen before. Jackie started crying and flew to the couch. Daddy hissed for both of us to be quiet and stay back. *No problem there!* I was on the couch beside my sister in a flash!

"Honey, what are we going to do?" my mother whispered anxiously. "You can't go out there! It will bite you! You will be late for work," she urgently continued as she ran to the kitchen broom closet.

I could tell Daddy was thinking the situation over. Back home in Michigan, we had non-poisonous garter snakes and blue racers that sometimes slithered into our yards. Rattlesnakes on the other hand were a whole different breed! For Daddy, there was no leaving to be done until that rattlesnake was no longer a threat. Protecting us was more important to him than punching a time clock. He was always real strict about being on time for work. Daddy and both of my grand-pas thought that the poorest example a working man could set for himself was being late to work, especially when you had just started a new job! They all had fired other people from their jobs for that very thing. But today, there was no leaving this scare for someone else to fix.

Mamma came charging back from the broom closet with the axe that daddy used to chop firewood when we cooked outside or built a campfire. She meant business! That ugly old snake had not moved an inch, which was surprising with the slamming of the trailer's screened door and all the running around that was taking place! I figured Daddy had slammed that trailer door just hoping that snake would take off to other parts. But nope! Not a chance! It just stayed put and didn't seem bent on going anywhere else.

Jackie and I were ever so thankful for that axe and its very long handle. Daddy kept the axe out in front of him as he slowly, inch by inch, started to swing the screened door full open. The snake had not moved from the spot where he had first been seen, coiled up on the second step of the trailer. I could see its head from where I was sitting. That rattler was sticking it way up to check things out. The head of the snake was moving from side to side trying to keep its beady black eyes on Daddy. Its tongue was darting in and out of its mouth. The rattle sound was loud and continuous now. The sound came faster as the outside screened door opened wider. Jackie and I were frozen to our spots and not moving off the couch! Mamma was clearly ter-rified as she stood far back, begging Daddy, in whis-pers, to do nothing except shut the door!

As Daddy started to slowly raise the head of the axe, faster than a blink that snake struck and flew two steps up into the doorway of the trailer, aiming for Daddy's leg, which was protected by the thick heavy boots that he wore every day to work. In an instant Daddy had brought the flat head of the axe down on the neck of that snake. The rattler had missed his mark, but Daddy hadn't. The snake was pinned beneath the axe. The handle of the axe was sticking straight up and Daddy was putting pressure on his push. Mamma's screams brought the neighbors running. Quickly, without hesitation, Daddy placed his big booted foot squarely behind the rattler's head and stepped down hard. Its long body was thrashing now, hitting the sides of the trailer doorway. Jackie and I were both crying, still on the couch, with our eyes open wide, and our legs pulled up under our chins! Jackie grabbed the couch pillow and was covering her eyes. Mamma commanded with a firm but trembling voice, "Girls, stay on that couch! Don't move an inch until I say!" as she ran to the back bedroom where Little Cathy had just awakened and was screaming loudly. Mamma grabbed Christie's hand on the way past. Sleepy-eyed, she had just walked into the hall, awakened from all the commotion. She was promptly dragged into the back bedroom on Mamma's heels and the door slammed shut behind all of them. *Oh, how I wish I was in that bedroom, too!*

Men from trailers nearby came running at all the commotion. Daddy was calling loudly to Sam, Mr. Domas, from across the driveway, as he got his paper from the box. Mr. Domas was there in an instant with an iron rake, the day's newspaper completely forgotten! From outside the trailer, Mr. Domas pressed the snake down hard with the rake on the top step leading into the trailer. He knew that my father was not letting that rattlesnake get away from under his boot. By that time, other men had come to help. Daddy handed the axe to Mr. Domas, as both men kept their grip on the rattler. Daddy slowly pulled the door partly closed so Jackie and I couldn't see Mr. Domas or the rest of the snake. We both knew what was coming next!

There was a loud **crack** of metal on metal twice and suddenly the snake stopped thrashing. Still Daddy didn't take his boot off of the snake. After many seconds of no movement from the rattler, Dad called to Sam to step away. As Daddy swung open the trailer door once again, Jackie and I could see the heads of our neighbors from the shoulders up, but they were not looking at us. They were watching intently for our father's next move. It was clear from their expressions that whatever had happened to that rattler was not pleasant! Using the toe of his work boot my father promptly kicked that snake right out the door, closing it quickly. Jackie and I burst into a full blown tearful melt-down, tore off the couch and ran into the back bedroom with Mamma and my sisters. We heard the trailer door shut tight behind Daddy as he exited. We stayed in the back bedroom with Mamma, begging her not to leave us, or open the door until Daddy came to give us the all clear! She started reading a chapter from one of our favorite books, Wind in the Willows, just to quiet us.

It only took a few minutes for Daddy to come and check on all of his girls. That rattler had given the whole family one unforgettable scare! He knew for sure that Mamma was upset, too as her eyes filled with tears when she saw him.

"Well the coast is clear! That old rattlesnake is as dead as a doornail!" Daddy reported much to our relief. "That nasty critter won't be curling up on anybody's trailer step again! Should've stayed where he belonged and maybe he wouldn't have ended up dead."

Jackie didn't miss a beat, "Daddy, can all of us go look at that 'nasty critter'?"

"Well, what do you think, Mamma?" Daddy responded looking directly at my mother. My mind was running in circles. *Is this really a good idea? I think I saw enough of that snake already, but.....maybe just one quick peek wouldn't hurt.*

"Do you really want to see that dreadful thing?" Mamma asked my sister with surprise. "You are all still shaking with the scare it gave you! We'll probably all have nightmares tonight!" She finished.

"Yes!" Came the reply in unison. Even Christie wanted a peek. Little Cathy not so much, she just shook her head NO. Finally Mamma relented and said we could see it, but only for a minute, and absolutely no touching it. *As if we ever would!*

To our surprise, when we stepped out of our trailer, there was a big circle of neighbors, including kids our age, standing around that 'dead as a doornail' rattlesnake. The cement slab beneath our steps was covered in blood. Daddy took a pail and washed most of it into the sand at the edge so you couldn't see it as much. The rattlesnake wasn't exactly cut in half, but looking at what was left of it made it easy to understand why it **was** dead! Mr. Domas' aim had been true! He was right on target. Everyone was talking, mostly in Spanish, and we had no idea what they were saying, but we could guess. One man was measuring the length of the snake. Another man picked it up just behind the head and pulled back the skin near its mouth so the fangs showed. We all backed up a few steps for that demonstration!

Mr. Domas and Daddy shook hands. They had worked together as a team and got the job done. Mr. Domas said it was one of the biggest they had seen in the park in quite some time. Everyone agreed that a snake like that was too dangerous to have around. You just never knew what might happen! Daddy and a couple of the neighborhood men took care of that old snake good and proper, and it didn't take long! Mamma made all of her girls go inside and miss the clean-up detail. But according to the story that Daddy shared later that night, our neighbors across the road, Mr. and Mrs. Gomez, who live beside Mr. Domas, had fried rattlesnake for dinner that very afternoon and loved it. *Yuck! How disgusting! How could anyone even think of eating such a thing?* Daddy said that lots of people eat rattlesnake and a person shouldn't find fault with it 'til they tried it themselves. *I am never trying it!*

For the first time ever, my dad was late to work. Wednesday was always popcorn night, but Daddy had to work overtime to make up for the hour and a half that he was late to work because of that mean rattler. Supper was late, so no popcorn that night! I appreciated the local wildlife even less after that episode. I can say for sure that I never opened that trailer door, even once after that day, when I didn't look out first to see just what might be sitting on our trailer steps!

Mamma had her own adventures getting to know people from the park. It always seemed to happen by accident; the way in which the neighbors took to accepting us as part of the trailer park neighborhood. A few of the women in the park, who lived in trailers near us, suddenly became friendlier the day after Mamma had quickly responded to the screams of a very young Latino mother.

A very young woman living near-by had her baby boy sleeping in a crib. The baby's bed was pushed against a wall, in the small motel room where the child's mother and father lived. The motel was just beyond the entrance drive into our trailer park. The terrified screams of the young girl brought my mother running.

Mamma bolted from the lawn chair in which she had been sitting, just outside our trailer door, shucking peas for dinner and folding laundry. She yelled for us to follow, as she scooped up my littlest sister from off the cement slab where Cathy had been sitting at my mother's feet. Following the screams, Mamma threw open the screened door to the tiny motel room. She handed my baby sister off to me, and went into the darkened room.

It took her eyes a few minutes to adjust from the blinding sunlight outside to the darker inside of the room. Slowly her eyes refocused to find a gigantic centipede crawling up the wall just above the baby's bed. It was huge! A black crawly thing with about one hundred legs! It must have been about a foot long; much bigger than any centipede Mamma had seen in Michigan! The young mother, who stood screaming at the foot of the bed, had lost all sense about what to do. She was startled out of her hysterics and reacted immediately when Mamma shouted, "GET THE BABY!" That's when the first time mother instantly grabbed her now screeching baby boy out of the bed, and ran out the door bawling her head off.

Without hesitation Mamma grabbed the broom by the door and started pounding on that nasty bug, like she was driving a nail into a board! My two youngest sisters watched with amazement as Mamma swung into action and took care of the situation in short order. After a good measure of pounding, she whisked that hideous, old thing off the wall and ran outside, with it still clinging to the broom. A man standing nearby, who didn't seem to be even one whit as brave as my Mamma, flicked his cigarette lighter onto the bottom of that broom and that ugly bug, along with the broom, went up in flames and smoke as fast as the snap of his finger. Mamma absolutely hates crawly creatures, and she loves babies more than anything. I knew that foot long critter was not having its way this time. Cathy, my baby sister, stood close by my side and cried through the whole ordeal, because she was afraid the bug would bite her or Mamma. *No need to worry on that count! Mamma made sure that wasn't happening.*

My mother walked over to comfort the young woman who was still crying softly and shaking from the scare. The baby settled right down as Mamma rubbed his back tenderly. He stared curiously at her as she spoke softly to him in words he probably had never heard before. English was not spoken as much as Spanish in these parts. After that day, several of the ladies started waving to Mamma when they saw her outside. They would smile and nod as we passed when the five of us were walking to the store around the corner, or just down the block to the Laundromat.

The day after the centipede scare, the baby's grandma, Mrs. Gomez, brought over a dish of Mexican tortillas rolled up with stuff in the middle and baked with cheese on top. At least it didn't look like rattle-snake! We were all relieved by that fact. The only Mexican food our family had ever eaten was Grandma's version of Spanish rice, which probably wasn't authentic Mexican food at all. As soon as Mamma put the plate down in front of her, Christie sat at the table crying 'til her eyes got all red. She just kept shaking her head "No" and wouldn't even try it. Jackie and I were certain that she was probably still worried it was rattlesnake. Christie had to settle for a peanut butter sandwich that night. Everyone else in our family thought the Mexican dish of beef chimmichangas tasted real good. Still, most of the time, we were just left to ourselves.

Chapter Eighteen

Herman Greene: The Albuquerque Cowboy

Like pirates with a treasure you might think about how to keep your new found friend all to yourself, so that you don't have to share your treasure with anyone. After all, you don't want anyone else playing with your forever friend, because they might like the other person better than you. That never works. Others recognize the value of what you have found, and the tighter you try to keep it, the more everyone else wants it. Share the treasure and everyone is happier. That makes you and your friend happier, too.

The first time I saw that boy, Herman Greene, he was wearin' long blue jeans with a scuffed up pair of brown leather cowboy boots sticking out from the bottom of them. Those boots were showing turned up toes which meant they were a little too long for his feet. *They were probably hand-me-downs from his brother, but then it looks like most everybody around here wears hand-me-downs, just like* **my** *littler sisters.* He had a tightly woven white straw cowboy hat sittin' atop a head of sandy brown hair the color of Wonder Bread toasted on the medium setting. No boy I had ever known wore clothes like his, except when they were dressing up like a cowboy for Halloween. *Now* **this** *was different.*

It was the shirt that caught my eye and kept me lookin' for longer than was polite. He must have known I was quite interested because he just stared right back, until I shyly turned away. His shirt was Easter grass green. Funny as I look back, given his name which I didn't know at the time. It was the decoration on it that I couldn't stop lookin' at, because I'd never seen a boy wear such a pretty shirt.

It was sewn with a brown cord between the collar and the third button, with pearl and silver-edged, round buttons at the cuffs, down the front, and at the points where the cord wove a lazy curved line across the front and back of that spring green shirt. *This boy knew how to dress! He looked like a real cowboy, just several feet too short.* The way I loved to watch cowboys in those T.V. Western shows, who could blame me for staring at a real live one just about my age.

He walked down the gravel road on the opposite side of the park trail that ran right past our lot. After we had that first look at each other, he never glanced my way again. He turned the corner at the first crossing and wandered out of sight. *Who was that kid?* My next younger sister, Jackie, looked at me but neither of us said, out loud, just what we were thinking although we knew. After a few minutes we continued playing our game of monopoly on the picnic table right outside our trailer door, and the boy in the Easter-green shirt was forgotten. In bed that night, just before sleep, Jackie said to me, "That cowboy sure must have been going to a fun party." We both laughed. It's funny how sisters sometimes think alike.

Early the next morning, Mamma was standing outside the trailer, behind the bench of the picnic table. I was sitting on the other side of the picnic table, across from where she stood brushing Jackie's long blonde hair. Mamma was getting ready to put my sister's waist length tresses up in the braids she wore almost every day. I was sitting at the table watching her and finishing my toast with grape jelly. *Yum!* Christie and Cathy were playing with their dolls on the trailer steps, pretending to feed them ginger snaps and windmill cookies for breakfast. My little sisters were getting the better part of those cookies. Mamma and Jackie were facing the opposite direction from me. Suddenly for no good reason, Jackie quietly kicked me under the table. "What?" I said, as she got my most serious, *you had better stop it or else,* glare. She motioned her head in the opposite direction that I was facing, but said nothing. She kept looking past the trailer, down the road.

"Jackie Sue, hold your head still." Mamma commanded. That was when I heard the crunch of stones and gravel coming in footsteps from behind me, getting louder with each step. I turned to see what caused Jackie to kick me so hard from under the table, and who or what was making the crunching steps that came closer and closer. All of us stared without apology or the slightest regard for offense.

What I saw when I turned around was just what I had expected from the look I saw on Jackie's face. There he was, same boy, same hat and boots, *same blue jeans maybe*, but a different shirt; navy blue and white plaid with short sleeves. This time a twisted, red colored cord ran down each side of his shirt. It started just under the collar and ran to the bottom of the shirt where it was neatly tucked into his jeans, just like yes-terday. This shirt had a small pocket on the right side with the head of a Texas Longhorn on it.

Sure enough that little cowboy was coming right our way, on our side of the trail this time, looking in our direction. Mamma stopped braiding. Jackie looked up. I kept my gaze in that direction. The crunching of his boots on the gravel road kept coming.

"Morning Ma'am, beautiful day ain't it?" he said quietly as he tipped his hat on his way past this family of newcomers to the neighborhood. *Oh my goodness, just like Matt Dillon from "Gunsmoke"! Mamma's gonna like this kid!*

"Well yes it is, Young Man, and don't you have some proper manners! Your Mamma teaches you well. You best be enjoying this fine day." Mamma answered cheerily.

"Yes Ma'am I sure will try," he answered politely as his steps slowed.

"What is your name?" She continued.

"My name's Herman Greene, Ma'am. Very pleased to meet you." The miniature cowboy complimented, as he quickly removed his hat, and a head of sandy-blond hair appeared. *Yep, Wonder Bread toasted just right.*

Mamma wouldn't let up, "Do you live around here? I believe I've seen you walking past our place before."

"Yes Ma'am, I do. Right 'round the corner just two blocks down, 142 Siesta Drive," was his very polite and informational answer.

I still can't peal my new address off that fast. I wonder how long he has lived in this park. Where'd he get manners like this?

"Herman Greene, it is very nice to meet you as well. These are my daughters: Terry, Jackie, (as she pointed to each of us in turn), and little Christie and Cathy there playing on the steps."

Mamma was on a roll. At least we wouldn't have to be introducing ourselves. She had taken care of all of that. *Whew! Thanks, Mom.*

She continued sweetly, "It appears that you might be nearly the same age as my two older girls. Perhaps on your way back this direction, you might want to stop for a cold glass of lemonade served right here at our picnic table? I just made it fresh this morning."

The way Mamma went on, she must have been tired of seeing us have no one to play with except each other. Who wanted to play with a boy you didn't even know? Not me!

"Well if it wouldn't put you out too much, that sounds mighty fine. The sun is sure to be heatin' things up today. Thank you again, Ma'am and I would surely enjoy that glass of lemonade on my way home." With that, Master Herman Greene placed his white straw cowboy hat back on his head, tipped it at the brim looking directly at my mother, and walked on down the road toward the corner store. Never looking my way even once!

Oh no, the hat tip...just like Matt Dillon on "Gunsmoke." Mom's a goner!

"My, what a nice young man he seems to be, and clean as a whistle," Mamma added after her farewell wave. *Oh bother! Mamma was definitely sold on this guy!*

Jackie and I weren't too sure about a boy who wore such fancy shirts, and had spotlessly clean fingernails. Not a speck of dirt under those nails anywhere. We both discreetly rolled our eyes at each other. *How did he manage that? Of course Mamma **would** like his clean looks and proper manners! A copy-cat of Matt Dillon, and Mamma had fallen for it...hook, line, and sinker! Yep, we just might be seein' more of Herman Greene than we had bargained for.*

Well, he sure did come back for a cold glass of that homemade lemonade, that day and for many days after. Once we got past that first meeting, Herman Greene, Jackie, and I were inseparable. We both admitted we liked his ways, especially how he talked. He had a slow southern drawl and the words just seemed to roll off his tongue. We all took turns laughing at each other, because he thought we talked funny, too. Every day he came by and we learned more things about what each of us liked and didn't. We played board games and catch. We played cards like Old Maid and War. We drew pictures of our favorite things. We learned about each other's families. Herman was always real nice to Christie and Cathy, and they adored him. He didn't have any brothers or sisters to give attention to so we thought he enjoyed our big family.

We played pretend games of Cowboys, which was easy for Herman, on account of him bein' one. We guessed that he was working at being just like his daddy, a real rodeo rider. Bronco riding and Brahma bull riding were Mr. Greene's specialties and you could tell when Herman talked about it, how proud he was of his daddy. That's why Herman's dad wasn't home much. He was on the road a lot going to different rodeos that were held in nearby cities and states. Sometimes Herman got to go with him on the road, but school and his mom's job, working at the dry cleaners, kept Herman at home. Bronco ridin' didn't always pay what they needed, so his mom kept her job to make the bills.

It was surprising to me how Mary Francis didn't seem to like the idea of Herman Greene one little bit. I tried to tell her the fun parts that Jackie and I liked about him, but she wasn't having it.

"What's that stupid idea of dressing like a cowboy every day?" She asked with contempt. "It's not

Halloween! I think that boy sounds awful, and I don't care how much Mom Cole likes his manners and polite ways!" She finished with a challenge, "Does that boy have a dog?"

"His name is Herman, Mary Francis." I said with exasperation. Her mention of a dog made me think of Lassie, and I was suddenly feeling homesick all over again.

Herman Greene always had some new adventure for us to go on. Mamma had him stay for lunch many days. He never seemed to have much of any other place to go, and it sure couldn't have been fun eating alone every day. His Mamma worked days and his daddy was just never home. Herman Greene seemed to be on his own most of the time. Mrs. Rogriquez lived next door to the Greenes and watched Herman when his mother worked. Mostly he just checked in with his older neighbor, or went over when he needed something. He seemed to like exploring 'round about and knew the area well.

The time we spent with Herman was never dull. He always thought up something interesting and fun to do. This Albuquerque cowboy sure loved Sky King, Sheriff of the Western Skies; a T.V. character that flew around in a single engine plane looking for bad guys. The two of them did seem to dress alike, with those fancy braided shirts and always a ten-gallon hat sitting atop their heads. One of Herman's favorite games to play was him pretending to be Sky King, with Jackie and me having to be the bad culprits he was after. He would pretend to show up in his plane just in the nick of time, proclaiming loudly the well-known T.V. jingle "Out of the blue comes Sky King" and then promptly dragged us off to jail. Our pretend prison was located near the backside of our trailer.

Even though we had already survived some terrifying run-ins with local wildlife, Herman introduced us to all sorts of Southwestern critters; creatures we had never seen around our home in Michigan. Cockroaches were a new nuisance for us to endure! They were everywhere. Mamma fussed daily about them. She set traps with poison at night trying to keep them under control. Jackie and I slammed them with shoes whenever we saw them and killed them every chance we got! Roaches are triple yucky! He taught us how to hold horned lizards in our hands and not be afraid. We learned how to stroke their heads so that they didn't run or try to escape the minute we had captured them.

Herman was an expert at spying stones that had special qualities. He showed us some interesting rocks that lay about and were common to the area. Jackie and I quickly added the most interesting ones to a collection we had started from some of the tourist stops we had visited on our way to New Mexico. Our collection would come to include rocks from the Badlands, the Grand Canyon, Mount Rushmore, and the cave where Jesse James and his brother Frank had holed up with the Hole in the Wall Gang. We thought our rock collection was real special and took every opportunity to add new and interesting pieces to it. Herman sure seemed to know where to find some good ones. But, forget the rocks, the most amazing thing he ever shared with us was the crawdads!

Chapter Nineteen

Not So Brave Yankee Girls

*How exactly **do** you know when you have found a best friend? Is it always peaceful and pleasant? Not a chance! Just ask Mary Francis or me. Don't think that you never have issues with a best friend. It is bound to happen.*

Maybe if those old crawdads had been christened with a different name it might have set better with all of us, especially Mamma. But that C-R-A-W part just set your teeth on edge and your mind on critters that crawl, and these sure did! Herman showed us a printed photograph of a crawdad in his "Southwest Dwellers" animal magazine. The beady eyes were bad enough, but the pincher proved to be the clincher! Herman Greene was real attached to crawdads and thought them to be the next best thing to cotton candy.

"You bein' Yankees and all," as Herman so often liked to say to us, "jist have no idea how interestin' crawdads can be. Maybe I'll show you a real one someday soon."

We thought that having crawdads for pets was stretching things a bit, but Herman's idea of considering such critters on the menu for lunch was beyond our understanding! Mamma turned white as a sheet at the mere suggestion of such a thing and my stomach felt like I'd just that minute stepped off from the highest and fastest Ferris wheel at the county fair.

Crawdad hunting was Herman's favorite past time. He could get an easy dollar for a dozen bait craw-dads. It cost his customers a dollar twenty-five if the critters were caught fresh that day and still lively enough, at the time of purchase, to be cooked for supper that night. Selling crawdads was how this little trailer park cowboy managed to earn extra money to buy a cold soda at the corner gas station on a hot day in New Mexico, which was almost every day. Hunting craw-dads was the one time Herman Greene got those clean white fingernails of his downright filthy, and he didn't care a whit. Herman's idea, of getting Mamma accustomed to crawdads, was doomed from the start due to poor planning on his part. It was the way in which he introduced us to them in the first place that was his undoing.

One hot August morning, with the sun already a huge ball of heat, hanging low in the sky, Jackie and I were walking back from takin' some fresh tomatoes to Mrs. Sanchez. Mamma had gotten fresh ones from the market the day before, and had more than she needed, so she asked us to run the extras over to one of our closest neighbors. With the tomatoes delivered as requested, Jackie and I were heading back to our yard. Herman came stomping up the bank from the creek that flowed behind the trailers on our side of the road.

It didn't take long for us to spy him totin' a long, narrow screen-covered box about the size of a fishing tackle box. His knees were brown with mud. Long dark streaks of thinned silt trickled down his legs to his feet, running back into the cracked earth clinging between his bare toes. Mud was caked on his arms clear to the elbows. His hands were stained a dark brown with mud dried on around his fingernails and lining the creases in his palms. *Strange, no cowboy boots on his feet this day. What was he up to? I sure hadn't seen him this dirty very many times.*

It was our intention to see what he was carrying in that box.

"What you carryin' in that old tackle box, Herman Greene?" Jackie asked.

"Your Mamma gonna' like that mud you got smeared all over your clothes? I quizzed. "What are you doing playin' around in the mud anyway?" I just had to know.

Herman shot a challenge right back at us, "If you want to prove that you really are the bravest of any Yankee girls I know, then you just might talk me into giving you one peek in this here box!"

Now Jackie Sue wasn't afraid of much. She could even put her own night crawler on the hook when she went fishin' with Daddy. (Those big, fat, slimy worms used for bait in Michigan had never been touched by **my** hands!) It was the scratchy, scritchy, clickity noises coming from the screen-topped box that was givin' her pause. Whatever was residing in that box, this very minute, was surely alive. *The question is how big and how dangerous? Does it bite? Is it one critter or more? Did alligators live out here in the west?* Our curiosity was getting the better of us and we were settled on seein' what was in that box!

"So...just what do we have to do to be proving our braveness and earn a peek?" Jackie asked cautiously.

"Promise y'all will do exactly as I say, and if you do what I am brave enough to do, y'all can have as many peeks inside this box as you want," Herman explained.

Jackie Sue and I walked a short distance away to talk this over. We both knew that Herman never did anything that required too much effort on his part. Also, being so courteous and well-mannered, his mamma must keep a close eye on him, certainly not allowing him to be too foolhardy about things. It sounded like a safe pact for us to consent to, so as to get our own prized peek.

We walked back the distance to where Herman stood patiently waiting our decision. He was smiling ever so innocent-like, which worried me a bit. *He wouldn't let something bite us...would he?*

Herman held up his free hand as if to stop us, "Before we shake hands to seal the deal, double swear, with no fingers crossed, not to look or open your eyes until I'm ready." He continued on "For sure no peeking 'til I give you the word that it's time to look. You have to do exactly the same thing that I do. Scouts honor!"

We should have known never to trust someone named Herman; who had no more sense than to live in a hot, dry, sandy place like Albuquerque, who made a hobby out of catching something called Crawdads, and used the word "y'all" way too much. Nevertheless, we swore the oath. We shook with no fingers crossed, and even sealed the deal with our secret handshake for good measure. (Clap-clap; shake hands; middle finger hand turn; hand slide; double snap.) We could still hear the click-clicks coming from the box as we finished the handshake ceremony. Herman had commanded both of us to stand with our eyes closed, with no peeking, which we did immediately. We could hear the top of the box open.

"No peeking!" he reminded. In another minute it opened again and closed for a second time. Then a third time and all was quiet for an instant.

"Okay, y'all open y'r eyes," he commanded in his familiar slow southern drawl.

With my nerves jangling, I wondered why his voice sounded so muffled. Well, we sure found out! Both Jackie and I, with great effort and uncontrollable squinching, opened our eyelids reluctantly out of fear for what was soon to be seen. Whatever we imagined as the worst possibility, could not have prepared us for the sight standin' before us now! Herman Greene, the newly named Crawdad Cowboy, stood there showin' a full set of white teeth behind the biggest smile anyone north of the Rio Grande ever saw. What our eyes beheld made our blood run cold and was too unbelievable to comprehend! Herman Greene was standing right in front of us with crawdads hanging from his face by their pinchers. One crawdad hung from each ear, and one from his nose! Those horrid creatures were wiggling their legs and holding on tight by their pinchers. Herman's eyes seemed to be watering. *They're eating him! Heaven Above, save us!* The bravest Yankee girls ever fell from grace in an instant.

One look was all it took! Later, there was a heated debate between us, as to which of 'The Bravest Girls' took to screamin' the loudest or ran away the fastest from that gruesome scene. My story was firm... Jackie ran away screaming at the top of her lungs, taking the lead in no time, with me on her heels. *How in the world would any cowboy in their right mind ever think for a second that two Yankee girls, no matter how brave, were going to repeat that disgusting display!*

On the first ear-splitting scream Mamma was at the trailer door searching out the reason for it. Her mouth was still formed in the words that didn't seem to come as we came sliding and skidding across the cement pad to the bottom of the trailer steps with Herman close on our heels! Mamma seemed like she was frozen in time as she swung open that trailer door without batting an eyelash. In we tumbled, all a pile of arms, legs, and tennis shoes. Mamma couldn't even get a word to come out as she stood staring speechless at Herman Greene, who was standing at the foot of the trailer steps in utter confusion with crawdads still hanging from his face. The slamming of the trailer door ended any deal that we were inclined to make that day with the Albuquerque (turned Crawdad) Cowboy.

This proved to be our first encounter with crawdads, but it wasn't to be the last! Though it wasn't the first time we ever **heard** of crawdads, it was the first time of **seeing** them that was the worst! Mamma met Daddy at the car that day, as soon as he got home from work. They talked at the car for several minutes. Mamma had told us to stay in the trailer, because we were to have no part of the discussion. Curiously Mamma kept wiping her mouth as she talked to Daddy with her back to us, as we watched the conversation going on between them. All of my sisters and I were kneeling on the sofa, staring out the front trailer windows. Daddy had a strange look on his face like when he strained to lift something heavy or tried hard not to do something he wanted to do... like laugh! Now that was confusing! *We could have been eaten alive by those crawdads! Nothing funny there!*

Daddy left in the car, drove down the road and turned onto Herman's street. Dad was back to the trailer by the time Mamma had set the table for dinner. After his hat was hung on the hook by the door, his work boots off and on the mat, Daddy got down to business. He looked at Jackie and me very seriously and shared what he had so recently been told.

"Mamma says you two had a run-in with some pretty nasty critters today. Guess we have to make sure that doesn't happen again. Both of you and Herman seem to have some talkin' that needs to be done. The sooner the better would be my way of thinkin' about it. We'll be takin' care of the whole matter after dinner is eaten. Herman will be comin' by." He turned on his heel and walked quickly into the bathroom, closing the door behind him.

Jackie and I just stared at each other. *Oh great! Just great! That nasty Herman Greene had better not be bringing any of those pinching, beady-eyed crawdad critters with him!* Neither of us ate much at dinner, or joined in the friendly chatter that always surrounded our table when we were at a meal. Our appetites were a bit off from the usual "clean your plate" routine.

Daddy had a quiet talk with Herman Greene outside the trailer after dinner the same night. Jackie Sue and I put our ears to the wall in our bedroom which was just above where the picnic table sat. We'd seen that on a spy show we had watched on television and it had worked pretty well. We strained to hear every word that was being said between the two of them as they sat at the table talking. We had been given strict orders to stay inside until Daddy called us out. We couldn't figure how Mamma didn't seem to care one fig about how Daddy would be giving it to that nasty Herman Greene! We could make out some low sounding "Yes, Sir" and "No, Sir" replies, but we were hopping mad when we could hear Daddy laughing real quiet and sounding all friendly to that pesky, short cowboy! He was saying something about us not caring for that style of jewelry, and being too young to wear earrings of any sort! Herman was laughing, too.

This was no joke, and we weren't seeing' anything funny in any of it. We could have dropped dead on the spot from the extreme amount of fear we were forced to endure just looking at that horrifying display! Daddy wouldn't have been laughing then!

Jackie and I set our sights on getting even then and there! We'd figure it out and Herman Greene was going to pay dearly for scaring the daylights out of us. My sister and I would hatch a plan and have our day to laugh at him! Yes Sir, we would show him!

Daddy called us out to speak with that crawdad cowboy who wore fancy shirts, "Teresa Lee, Jacquelyn Sue, front and center." We always reacted immediately when Daddy used our given names. It was always hop to it and come when you are called, because when Daddy used that tone, he meant business. Jackie and I came at Daddy's command, but we didn't like it one little smidge! Herman Greene made his apologies very politely to my sister and I, and we accepted them somewhat begrudgingly. We both sat there silently still punishing Herman for his mean ways in scaring us so badly. Daddy just kept on chattering away like there wasn't the littlest thing wrong.

Daddy got out the Monopoly game after the little girls were in bed. We played until dark. The game began with a tense start. Jackie quickly chose the cowboy hat to be her playing piece for the game, so that Herman couldn't have it. He never said a word. It was the one he **always** picked as his play piece. Jackie always liked the cowboy boot for her playing piece, but she had chosen Herman's piece just out of spite. Herman took the cowboy boot tonight, and I thought that Jackie wasn't quite sure if that worked out the way she wanted it. Mamma wouldn't have liked Jackie's bad manners in not letting company choose first, but Daddy never mentioned it and Mamma wasn't there at the moment. I was glad he didn't have his way, and I told Jackie so, just before we drifted off to sleep that night. The Monopoly game ended on a peaceful note. We were into the thrill of winning and the trials of the day were forgotten, at least for now.

The next day was like any other day and we were compadres once more. Jackie and I did think it very curious how Herman Greene, now the Crawdad Cowboy, never brought those mangy critters around again, or even spoke of them, which relieved us greatly. No matter how many times Jackie and I discussed it, we never quite figured out Herman Greene's sudden lack of interest in his beloved crawdads, with him being so fond of them and all.

Chapter Twenty

Sunset at Sandia Crest

This year was our first time of not being with Grandpa and Grandma on the Fourth of July. We would surely be missing Grandma's potato salad and home-made lemonade, a yearly tradition in the celebration of honoring our country's birthday and Old Glory. Also, none of Grandma's coconut cake with the flag stuck in the middle. Another anticipated part of the holiday that we looked forward to every year. Fireworks at the county park, back in Michigan, wouldn't be a part of life this year either. Life felt downright miserable as we muddled through living in this dried up, brown state we now called home.

Daddy seemed determined to make the best of it, and had heard about the fireworks the county fired off at the top of Sandia Crest, a table-top plateau, located a few miles outside of Albuquerque. The trek up the mountain was a steep climb by car on the switch-back roads that traversed in criss-cross fashion, up the front face of the plateau. No guard rails protected careless drivers from a deep plunge off the edge onto the rock hard desert floor hundreds of feet below. Small white crosses marked the places along the side of the road where unlucky drivers had lost their lives from "drive-overs." No one survived the falls from any distance above the second switchback.

Our travels through the Rocky Mountains had been our first glimpse of those white crosses that sent shivers down your spine upon seeing them, and marked the roads along a traveled path that proved treacherous even on good days of driving with no rain or snow to make the way even more perilous. Sandia Crest certainly was not as high as the Rocky Mountain chain, but it was the highest geographical point on the horizon that bordered a flat land of sand, scrub brush, and tumbleweed. It took about forty minutes of driving from the bottom of that plateau to the tippy-top, which wasn't tippy at all, but very sturdy, on account of being made out of solid rock! Nevertheless, there were moments when it felt very scary while my sisters and I rode along in the car, looking over the edges of some of those road shoulders that came way too close for comfort. Then as always, the white crosses as a reminder to keep white-knuckled drivers from losing their concentration, for even one moment!

So this year, yet another new experience notched the string of a whole line of new experiences that had come to fill our days since we had left Michigan. This one would be fireworks on Sandia Crest. Mamma packed a picnic supper and we left mid-afternoon to start our trek up to the plateau; a fixture in the land-scape that we looked at everyday just beyond our trailer park perimeter. We had watched some beautiful sunsets with great expectation, as Mother Nature artis-tically painted Sandia Crest in the dusk of the evening sky. A huge sphere of changing color, our sun would take its time sinking behind the city's naturally made rock monument. We thrilled in the fiery colors (red, yellow, orange, pink and purple) that splashed the face of Sandia Crest and were majestically thrown against the ever constant azure sky. The very same sky which seldom brought any cloud to provide even the smallest drink of watery rain; something that this parched land longed for each and every day.

Herman's dad had gone to a rodeo that week. It was a benefit event to raise money for a Native American reservation nearby that needed financial assistance for the tribal school. Many of the cowboys on Mr. Greene's rodeo circuit donated one weekend a year to ride for a favorite charity. This was the event Herman's father favored. Herman's mamma had to work all week, and so they stayed at home for the Fourth, leaving Mr. Greene to make this road trip alone. Mrs. Greene was tired from working all week and more than happy to allow Herman to accept my father's invitation to join us for our Fourth of July trip to Sandia Crest. She knew from past experience that Herman would be well cared for when he was with us. Herman always enjoyed himself and spent a generous share of his days at our trailer. His mom knew that he would have a good time, because he always seemed happiest whenever we were together.

Finally, Mamma had our picnic supper packed and loaded, along with the folding lawn chairs packed in the back end. She included a colorfully woven Indian serape blanket for keeping us warm or offering something soft to sit on. Mamma had bought it from a Native American vendor she had seen along the roadside as we travelled west. Eventually, the last box for our picnic was loaded.

Four little Cole girls and Herman Greene piled into the back seats of our 1957 black Ford station wagon. The whole family sang patriotic songs as we wound our way up the mountain, following in a long line of cars that never seemed to end. Each of us got a turn to pick the next song, even the Albuquerque/Crawdad Cowboy. Herman got to go first because he was company; the unspoken rule when it came to having guests. We all sang his favorite, "The Yellow Rose of Texas", three times.

Daddy finally parked the car on the top of the mountain. Due to the heavy traffic, the trip had taken close to two hours; more than double the time it usually took to reach the top of the plateau. The place was packed with people. Local citizens were everywhere, sitting on blankets, eating picnic suppers, listening to car radios, playing cards, or sitting quietly conversing with neighbors. Everyone was waiting anxiously for the big fireworks event.

Herman was enjoying his share of the picnic supper, and never saw the softball coming his way! He ducked, but not quickly enough! His nose was spurting blood all over his plate of food which didn't look as appetizing in red! Mamma and Daddy both swung into action. Mamma grabbed a towel she had brought to wipe off sticky hands and mouths. Daddy leaned Herman back and held pressure on the top of his nose until the bleeding started to slow a bit. A man nearby, who happened to be a doctor, came over to inspect Herman's suddenly crooked and still bleeding nose. The helpful doctor announced shortly that indeed Herman's nose had been broken when the softball hit him in the face. He continued by saying that Herman should have it looked at by his own doctor, as soon as possible.

Daddy said "There's nothing to be done about it tonight, on account of it bein' a holiday. Seein' a doctor will have to wait 'til tomorrow at the earliest." So, Mamma put some ice, from the thermos of lemonade, in the corner of the tablecloth and held it on the top of poor Herman's rather crooked nose. At least the bleeding had stopped by now, and Herman was feeling somewhat better, but his eyes just kept watering from the whole ordeal.

Dad and Mamma asked Herman if he wanted to go home, and forego the fireworks. He instantly shook his head "No," though very slowly and carefully (due to his throbbing nose and face). With painful effort and a slight nod to my parents he continued, "Sir, Ma'am, I sincerely thank you both for your kind concern regardin' my busted nose. I am feeling a might better now. I've been waitin' for this all week, so I'd like to be stayin' if it's all the same to y'all. I'd sure appreciate seein' some fine fireworks tonight, that is if y'all don't mind?"

I could hear Mamma mumbling quietly, "Well, if he is not the politest young man that I have ever met, I will eat my words! For heaven's sake... and with a broken nose no less!" *Yep, she sure thought his manners were "the best thing since sliced bread!"*

Mamma decided quickly that this was precisely the right moment to surprise us all with the special coconut cake that she had secretly baked to celebrate our first Fourth of July in a new place. When she stuck the small American flag in the middle, we all cheered our approval. *I believe that cake may have tasted even better than Grandma's.*

We lit up the sparklers Daddy had brought home from work that Friday. Our little hand-held lights glittered the darkening sky. I wondered what that looked like from the valley floor. Did the people looking up toward the top of Sandia Crest see all the little fire-lights that we were creating? The sparklers reminded me of the fireflies in Michigan. On hot August nights they twinkled in the brakes and bushes and lit up the evening darkness. It was as if a thousand little twinkling stars celebrated the occasion while we all waited for coming darkness and the fireworks to begin.

I'm not sure how much any of us really enjoyed them, because the fun seemed to have gone out of all of us after Herman's tangle with that softball. The boy who threw it felt the worst of anyone. He had come right over just after it all happened. He stood wringing his hands, and apologizing over and over about how he never meant for that ball to come flying over in our direction, but had to admit that his aim had been off.

He kept repeating the same question, "Are you all right? Are you all right?" I felt like screaming!

No he's not all right, you bone head! Look at his nose! Look at the blood! Does that look all right to you?! Thanks to you, his nose looks like one of the switch-backs going up Sandia Crest! And by the way, thanks also for totally ruining our entire Fourth of July! But of course I didn't, because Daddy and Mamma would have had my hide for being so impolite to someone who was clearly sorry for the accident he had caused. *Oh goodness, my words* **were** *sounding like a Mary Francis retort. She was definitely rubbing off on me. Besides, that baseball player-wanna-be looked miserable enough for everybody.*

While Mamma kept the ice to Herman's nose, Jackie came over and whispered in my ear..."I think Herman Greene, Albuquerque Cowboy and Crawdad King, just got the payback he deserved for scaring us with those nasty old crawdads. I think we should just let him be when it comes to getting even." I grudgingly agreed, because it looked as though his poor nose was never going to be the same!

I looked at Herman Greene, with that pretty cowboy shirt all covered in blood. It was not hard to decide, that indeed, I had gotten my revenge in a most unexpected way. Somehow it didn't feel one bit good either! I didn't even have a hand in it, for which I was most glad. There was no joy in seeing him hurt like

TERESA LEE

this. In fact, I felt deep down terrible about the whole thing and had to admit to myself honestly: *If getting even meant hurting someone, then I was done with any thought of doing such a thing. After all, no one likes to see a cowboy cry.*

Herman was taken to the doctor the very next morning. My dad drove Mrs. Greene and Herman to the office. The doctor straightened Master Greene's nose, which caused Herman a good share of pain for a few days following the visit. There was still a little bit of a crook in the line of his nose, but it was greatly improved over the way it had looked just after the ball smashed it sideways! He didn't feel much like visiting or playing for the next week, but he was going to be all right. That was something all of us were happy about.

You know, I never did get that picture out of my mind of those ugly crawdads decorating the face of one small handsome cowboy. Herman Greene had become more of a friend than I ever cared to admit, but Mary Francis was still number one!

Chapter Twenty-One

The Best News Ever, I Think?

Grandpa Jackson often reminded, "True friendship stands the test of time even when you're old or one of you dies. You still think of each other and smile, sometimes through a tear. You see, you're always grateful for the treasure of a best friend."

It's generally agreed that older people are wise and know the score. They talk true. So, when it came to advice on friends, we mostly listened and tried to remember.

*Mary Francis said, "If you don't believe what **THEY** say, then good luck finding the Yellow Brick Road that leads to The Emerald City." We loved the "Wizard of Oz"!*

Summer was moving on quickly. The August heat in New Mexico was unbearable most days. We stayed inside in the air-conditioning for the better part of late morning and for certain all afternoon. People didn't get out and about 'til the sun was lower in the sky. Mamma seemed quieter as the days passed, and her laugh didn't come as easy. Daddy was having his own worries at work, and seemed more tired at the end of his day. The start of school was still a ways off, but that was another hurdle to jump. It just seemed that life was becoming more complicated and I worried about the creased lines that appeared more often in my parents' foreheads when they were discussing their day or paying the bills.

Things just didn't seem to be going that well for my dad at work. Daddy didn't want to take the breaks that so many guys at work took regularly. He wanted to get his eight hours in and get home as soon as he could. It was a union shop so everyone had to take the prescribed breaks, and the standard lunch period. Dad thought there was a lot of wasted time in an eight hour shift. The new job required that a certain number of cupboards be produced in one day. The new method was to glue the joints and seams that held the cupboards together. Daddy wanted to put in a screw or nail when the cupboards didn't fit just right or the glue didn't seem to hold tightly enough due to a warp in the wood. A line boss had told him that he couldn't make his cupboards that way, because all the cupboards produced had to be made with the same degree of workmanship. Daddy didn't take well to that kind of thinking. He took pride in his work and the product that he turned out. He was just as fast as the other guys. He just did a better job of putting the same cupboards together. He had already been given a warning that he had to use only the glue: No nails, no screws, regardless of the way they fit together.

The argument the company gave was that if a buyer saw that some cupboard units were put together in a more quality way, they might get mad and start questioning the company. Those kinds of complaints were not good for business. So the policy was, follow the assembly routine as directed, no special attention, no matter what. In other words, do a mediocre job so that all the cupboards were the same. That had never been the way Daddy operated. It certainly was not the way his reputation for superior work had been earned when he owned his own business. Really, he didn't know any other way.

School was to be starting in several weeks. Mamma and Daddy were beginning to ask around about the schools. They would take us for rides on Sundays to drive past different schools in the area. Daddy had not been pleased with a visit he had made to the school nearest to where we were living. It was not what we had been used to at Robert Kerr School. Most of the kids attending the school spoke Spanish, as well as the teachers. It was sometimes difficult to understand what they were trying to say in English. Daddy was worried that we might not be able to understand what the teacher was instructing. The schools were made out of adobe. No air conditioning. Due to the heat, the school year was shorter than what we had been used to, with almost no time off for holidays. The cockroaches and rats were about those buildings more than my parents cared to see. It was a constant worry for my mother. She was set on us having the best situation when it came to our schooling. Jackie and I didn't even like thinking of being in any other school except Robert Kerr. I was ever so happy that school was still some weeks off. The whole idea of starting in a new school was scary.

One day in late August, Daddy came home from work around lunch time. He never did that! As soon as he pulled into the driveway, Mamma opened the door to the trailer, as a worry line creased her brow. She watched as my father stepped from the car with his lunch pail in his hand. She followed his slow steps across the cement pad to the trailer steps. As Daddy came up the steps, Mamma moved aside to let him pass, with an obvious question in her eyes, but not saying a word. Daddy took a quick look about; Jackie, Christie, and I were still sitting at the kitchen table, finishing our egg salad sandwiches from the lunch that Mamma had made for us. Cathy had finished and was playing on the floor with her doll. Mamma had been ironing all morning, so the ironing board was still up in the living room, with the iron still hot. Daddy walked over to the table, opened his lunch pail, sat down beside Jackie, and started to eat his lunch, without so much as a "How's your day going?" or flashing his usual smile.

Mamma came and stood by his chair. "Honey, why are you home for lunch? Was there a lay-off at the shop? Are you feeling sick? Did you get hurt? What's going on?" Her questions tumbled out.

Daddy looked around the table at each of us, and then he looked directly up at my mother. "Who wants to go back to Michigan to live?"

Without a moment's hesitation my sisters and I all screamed in unison, "WE DO!" Mamma never said a word, as her eyes filled with tears, and she threw her arms around my father's neck and cried happy tears all over his sawdust covered work-shirt.

"Well good and glad to hear it, because I quit my job this morning! I refuse to glue one more cussed cupboard!" my father finished by slamming his fist on the table for emphasis. "It just ain't right never usin' a nail when you're buildin' cupboards for folks."

The room exploded into joyful chaos, filled with dozens of questions from four little girls. When would we leave? *Jump, jump.* How long would the trip back take us? *Jump, twirl.* Could we call our Grandpas and Grandmas right away to tell them the good news?

Hug, jump. What about starting school? *Clap, clap.* On and on the questions spilled. After a few minutes Daddy held up his hand to stop the constant chatter and commotion coming from each of us.

"Now just a minute here, I haven't heard one word from your mother yet," Daddy said with a smile on his face.

Mamma turned a beaming smile toward him, with tears still clinging to her eyelashes. "When do I start packing?" she grinned.

"The sooner, the better I'd say." And he kissed her firmly on the mouth, as together they both started laughing. My sisters, and I jumped around for almost an hour with tears of joy filling our eyes and generous hugs given freely. Mamma even joined our celebration as she and Daddy danced around the living room while we laughed together louder and longer than we had in a very long time.

We called Grandpa and Grandma just about dinner time to be sure that they would be home. We could hear Grandpa's loud whoop from our seats on the couch, as Mamma held out the phone for all of us to enjoy his reaction. Grandma cried through most of the conversation. It was plain to my sisters and me, that they were as happy as we were that our days in Albuquerque, New Mexico, a state much too far away, were almost over. We'd be home within two or three weeks.

It was the call to Mary Francis the next morning that put a smile on my face that didn't come off for the rest of the day. Their phone was ringing before 8:00 A.M. so that her parents would still be at home and not gone off to work yet. Before Mary Francis came to the phone, my mother filled Mrs. Carson in on the news and asked her to let me be the one to share it with

Mary Francis. My very sleepy, best friend came to the phone, and uttered a strangled, "Hullo? This is Mary."

"I know who this is! Remember, I called you," I quipped.

"Terry, why are you calling me so early? I was sleeping, and we just talked on Monday," she whined.

"Don't be such a baby! I have something to ask you," I countered.

"What? So ask away, I'm hungry," she persisted.

"O.K., O.K. What are you having for breakfast?" I played.

"You called me from New Mexico to ask me what I'm having for breakfast?" she was beginning to sound a bit testy.

"No, I was calling to see if you wanted to have a slumber party in two weeks?" I said in the most innocent voice I could muster.

"What? Is your mom there? Does she know that you are running up a phone bill asking me stupid questions? Are you sleep-walking?" Mary countered with concern in her voice.

"YES. YES. And NO," I returned.

"And just how do you think we can have a slumber party? I don't fly you know, and neither do you!" She was definitely not considering all the options.

I could hear her mother in the background saying, "Mary, don't be so sassy."

"Well, I know how much you love sleepovers. So, I thought that when we get back in about two weeks, we could have one," I said very nonchalantly.

Dead silence on the other end. *O.K., it's finally sinking in!*

"Hello?" No response. "Hello-o-o?"

"What are you saying?" came the squeak from the other end. "School will be starting! You have to be at your school. You can't miss the first day! No one does that!"

"I will be at my school. My **new** school in Michigan! WE ARE COMING HOME! Home to stay! Home for good!" The happy tears were in my trembling voice as I finished.

What followed was a deafening scream from Mary Francis, and then she was crying too. My ears rang for hours afterward, from the pure joy that emitted from that screech. Don't ever let anyone tell you that you can't **hear** joy! You certainly can. I heard it that day. She had the same reaction that my sisters and I had. Her questions were tumbling out, one after another. I couldn't answer most of them, but she didn't care. It was enough to know that we wouldn't be two thousand miles apart anymore, and we'd be seeing each other on a regular basis. The slumber party was going to happen again and again, and that's what mattered most. We'd be together, sooner than we ever imagined, and all that we had hoped for in our prayers and in our dreams and in every thought we had of each other was about to be real again. Back where we belonged, with all the people that loved us best.

Chapter Twenty-Two

Last Good-byes

Reverend Griswold and Father Matt preached in summer bible school, "True friends help each other to become the best they can be. Best friends are one of God's greatest blessings." I sure believed what they had to say being ministers of The Word and all.

It's a funny thing how moving takes on a whole different happy color when you are moving back HOME! No tears, no complaining about all the work of packing, no whining about what is being left behind, only great anticipation for all the reunions soon to be enjoyed. Leaving Albuquerque, New Mexico was not going to be hard. After all, we had only lived there a little more than four L-O-N-G months!

However, leaving a small cowboy named Herman Greene would be a whole different thing. Isn't it strange how when you've bumped into the right person, it seems like you have known each other forever, even when you haven't. It's like you know what their heart is speaking even before either of you open your mouth.

Jackie and I would sometimes argue over who Herman liked better. We both agreed we liked him equally and he must have felt the same about us. At least that was the idea that kept the peace. I wondered too, if I might marry that ole' crawdad-lover someday. When Daddy came home sayin' we were headed back to Michigan, I knew it wasn't to be, but we all sure had taken a liking to each other.

How could moving back home, something I had earnestly wished for and mentioned in my prayers every night, be coming true, and me be feeling sad about some little piece of that wonderful happening? It seemed downright ungrateful to the Good Lord after him having heard my pleading prayer and answering it. I remembered Grandma saying, "Be careful what you wish for, 'cuz sometimes you get stuff that goes along with it that you'd wish you hadn't." Now I knew what she meant by those words. It would not be easy saying good-bye to Herman Greene no matter how excited I was to be going back home. What would Herman say when he found out? By now, he seemed to be just as attached to us as we were to him. Jackie, Herman and I had been inseparable ever since that first week of getting to know each other and all our particulars; like our favorite gum, favorite cartoon show, favorite animal to draw, favorite board game and on and on.

Playing games that we made up was one of our favorite past-times. We would keep at our watermelon seed spitting' contests 'til the sun had been long down and we couldn't even see whose seed was landing closest to the partial piece of string laid down for the finish line. Herman and Daddy had gotten us started with that game, even though Mamma didn't approve of young ladies spitting in public.

She said, "Just isn't fitting for any girl brought up with proper manners to be doing such a thing, especially out in broad daylight where everyone can see!"

Daddy just laughed and suggested, "Honey, why don't you use this chance and take a rest. Maybe you could read a book to the Little Girls, until the game is over?"

Mamma followed Daddy's suggestion, but didn't act like she was all that enthused about his idea of reading a story just then. She grumbled all the way down the hall to the back bedroom, with the Little Girls trailing behind her, each clutching a book.

The score was tied and we were finishing what we had started the night before. I don't know who liked this game more, the dad or the kids! Anyway, we sure had fun spittin' those seeds. Who would Herman spit seeds with after we abandoned him for Michigan?

The day we had to tell Herman the news, neither me nor any of my sisters looked forward to dropping the big bomb! Our minds swam with all sorts of confusing thoughts and concerns: *Would our very own cowboy cry? Cowboys don't cry do they? We'd sure never seen one cry on T.V. Matt Dillon, sheriff of Dodge City and Davy Crockett never cried! We certainly had not seen Herman shed a single tear, excepting when he broke his nose and his eyes started watering from a dust speck he said he got in there when the ball hit him square in the face. What would we do if he DID cry?* We didn't want to know, and we sure better not cry in front of him, on account of us being the bravest Yankee girls he ever knew, exceptin' when it came to crawdads. Any way you looked at it, no easy time would come from having to say good-bye to our Albuquerque, Crawdad Cowboy.

Daddy quit his job at the cabinet factory on a Friday. The Sunday following, we were all out in the yard after supper talking about the news of our move. The Greene's came driving past and stopped for a minute to talk. We immediately ceased our "moving" conversation when they pulled up alongside the road. Daddy started in asking Herman's dad how the rodeo had gone that weekend, and they chatted away. Herman's dad had taken a second place trophy in Brahmin bull riding. Jackie and I didn't know exactly what that meant, but Daddy said it was one of the toughest and most dangerous events at the rodeo. We did know that was one bright, shiny trophy that Mrs. Greene held up for us to see. Herman showed us his new apple red cowboy hat, and the play gun with a holster that he had gotten as a souvenir. They were all so excited about the good turn of events at the rodeo, no one dared mention our news. It could certainly wait one more day.

As the Greene's began to climb back into the truck that they always drove to rodeos, Mamma quickly invited all of them over to share supper with us the very next day. It was plain that she intended to tell our news then, and not put it off any longer. Maybe that was best. It was a jolt, like a bolt of lightning' striking the barn, when we realized that we probably didn't have many picnic lunches left to enjoy here at the trailer park with Herman Greene.

Mary Francis and I talked on the phone for a few minutes the very next morning. She was getting ready to go shopping with her mother for a new pair of saddle shoes for school. We both hated having to wear those clunky old things just because moms thought they were good for your feet!

Mary had questions on her mind and cut straight to the point, "What did that boy, Herman Greene, you're always talking about, have to say about your moving back?"

TERESA LEE

"He doesn't know yet. His family is coming over tonight for a cook-out. Daddy and Mom are telling them then," I explained.

"Woo-Eee, is he going to be surprised! Not that I care or anything... but still... jeepers-creepers!" Mary finished with a quieter, more considerate tone.

"Yes, I think he'll be very sad." I added.

There was silence on the other end of the phone for several seconds.

"Well, I hate to admit it, but I'm sorry for him. I'm happy for me, for all of **us**, but I'm sorry for Herman. It hurts bad, real bad!" Mary finished with a quiver in her voice.

That Mary Francis could be real loveable when she tried.

It had been one of those unbearably hot Albuquerque days. Mamma decided it would be hamburgers on the grill for dinner, so that she didn't have to heat up the stove. She had made her homemade biscuits for the strawberry shortcake early in the morning so her baking would be done before the day turned off hot. The Greene's arrived right on time, and we all shared a cooling glass of lemonade with lots of ice! It sure tasted good. On hot days like this, most people didn't seem to have the big appetites they enjoyed on cooler days. Still, it's hard to beat a hamburger deluxe with fresh garden picked tomatoes sticking out on every edge and dribblin' down your chin with each yummy bite.

It appeared like dessert was going to be not so sweet tonight, as Daddy began the story that was sure to hold the news of our move. While Mamma put the last of the whipped cream on the strawberry shortcake, Jackie and I sat with our eyes glued to the red and white checked tablecloth covering the picnic table. The Greene's all sat quietly and listened as the story of us moving back to Michigan unfolded, but none sat more still than Herman.

Mamma had fixed strawberry shortcake with whipped cream because it was one of the favorite things Herman had liked to eat at our house. She passed the dishes around as Daddy continued to talk. After each had been served, everyone except Herman started to eat the beautiful dish of dessert set down in front of them. Daddy had just finished the part about us starting to pack so that we could leave within a week or two, and be back in Michigan only a few days after the start of school there. The table was silent. No voice broke the irritation of the jay screaming from the tree at the back of the trailer. I peeked up from my first taste of whipped cream and saw Jackie looking straight at Herman. His head was down and his spoon was still on the table.

Herman drew in a quivery breath and looked straight at my dad. "Mr. Cole, do ya' suppose you could use some help every day loadin' up that trailer? I sure would be obliged if y'all allowed me to help." I could see that Mrs. Greene had tears in her eyes.

Mr. Greene reached over and patted Herman on the back. "I think that is a mighty fine offer, Son. And it's sure likely that Mr. Cole will get to see just what a good worker our boy can be when he's helpin' out."

"Herman" my dad responded, "I know for a fact that I couldn't possibly do it all without your help. Thanks so much, it was mighty kind of you to offer. There should be lots of strawberry shortcake for rewarding hard work, the likes of which will be dished out generously. Right, Mrs. Cole?" Daddy asked Mamma.

"I do believe that strawberry shortcake has a way of reviving even the hardest of workers," Mamma replied with a smile. "I will make sure that we have plenty."

All the grown-ups laughed. The younger ones around the table kept looking one to the other. Cathy, my littlest sister who was still only four, perked up and said to Herman, "We love you, Herman Greene. Same as you love Mamma's strawberry shortcake." We couldn't help but laugh a little at her honesty. Finally, there it was. An ever so slight tug upward at the corner of Herman Greene's mouth, almost a smile.

Still, he finished only half of his strawberry short-cake. I'd never known him to leave a dish of it only half eaten. *Truth be told, I wasn't very hungry either.*

Just to be polite, Mamma promised to keep the rest of it for him tomorrow if he wanted to stop by. He said he thought he might. I knew he would! I didn't sleep well that night, and I knew that Herman wasn't sleeping either. We would talk it out tomorrow. I hoped that he wouldn't be too sad with us going, but I knew in my heart that he would, because I felt deep down lonesome already, and we weren't even gone.

For the next week, each day, Herman helped Daddy. They would gather more stuff, which Mamma had boxed up, and then pack it into the silver pull-along trailer. Item by item the house trailer began to empty out and the tires on the little trailer seemed to sag more everyday under the weight of it all. I thought it was a little like Herman's spirits. On Monday he was still laughing and joking with Daddy and wanting to play games with Jackie and me when the work was done. By Friday, he was quiet and didn't seem to want to do much of anything. Mamma still gave him the strawberry shortcake, which seemed to make him feel better. We would be leaving on the coming Monday morning bright and early, just like always. With only a few days left, I didn't want to miss a thing, but Herman was just not himself, the play had gone out of him.

On Saturday morning, Mamma had made some cinnamon rolls for us to eat out at the picnic table after we finished our Rice Krispies and toast. Herman came riding up on his bike.

"Herman, come and have a sweet roll with us," Jackie invited with excitement.

"No thanks, I'm not hungry," his reply. "I'm heading over to Juan's for a game of catch," Herman ended in an uninterested tone.

"Well then you just go ahead and do that!" my sister snapped back. "I hope you can smell the pure goodness of this delicious cinnamon and brown sugar sticky bun with every step, because you won't be getting one of these at JUAN'S! So you just go right ahead and keep wasting every minute we have left pouting around about it, **instead** of having fun **with us**!"

Wow! My eyes popped open wide and so did Herman's. I had never heard Jackie speak to him this way. It was clear we were all trying to deal with this whole idea of leaving and doing it differently! We were in new territory and not really knowing what exactly to do or say.

"Well now, don't you seem a little testy today, Miss Jackie?" Herman shot back.

"Yes I am and what are you gonna do about it?!" She countered. This was not my sister's usual approach to pesky acting boys. She usually rolled her eyes and walked away without a word when a boy started being unreasonable. It was true, once Jackie Sue got riled up you best take a step or two back. I think she had learned a lot from watching Mary Francis effectively handle sassy boys in our neighborhood. However, it did seem to be working. Herman stood stuck to that spot, without moving. He leaned on the handle bars of his bike, looking down at the stone covered road, and seemed to be thinking over all that she had just spewed out at him.

He looked up at us from above the handle bars with his jaw set in a straight line, beginning softly and ending with conviction, "I see your point, but it doesn't mean I like it one little bit!" He snapped.

"Well, neither do we! Right, Terry?" came Jackie's quick comeback.

"We don't like leaving you behind any more than you like us going. I hate losing even one more minute of fun together. We don't have much time left you know?" I finished.

"I guess one cinnamon roll wouldn't hurt before I go over to Juan's," Herman hesitated.

He parked his bike quickly and sat down at the table. Between mouth-watering bites of our cinnamon rolls, we began talking about the tiny horned lizard that Christie had caught with Mamma's dust rag. Christie ran to get the jar that she had put her little lizard in for safe keeping until Herman came by our place. She could hardly wait to show it to him. All thoughts of the edgy conversation we had just shared were forgotten.

Herman never went to play catch that day with Juan. We spent the afternoon doing all the things we enjoyed most, which of course, did not include playing with crawdads. We picked up sparkly desert rocks to add to our collection. We walked the ditch looking for frogs and **small** snakes. We played marbles in the sandy side lot, and finished with a card game of Crazy Eights at the picnic table. Herman stayed for supper and we roasted hot dogs over a fire in the grill. It was our last full day of play. The end here was coming much too fast now. Everyone was feeling it.

We spent the rest of the day together until the sun went down behind Sandia Crest and the sky turned to a burnt-orange as the night colors washed it away with the darkening dusk. We talked and laughed together, trying to forget about the leaving. Finally, well after my little sisters had been shuffled off to bed, Mamma announced it was time for our "goodnights." Daddy walked Herman home, as Jackie and I watched their backs disappear into the darkness. The dim lights on the side of the trailer helped hide the tears that stung my eyes at the sight of their going.

Sunday afternoon many of the surrounding neighbors came to say their good-byes. It seemed that most everyone in the park knew that the family with the four little blonde-headed girls would be leaving on Monday. The Greene's came together as the sun was sinking in the afternoon sky. Mamma had invited the Greene family to come in out of the day's heat for a cold glass of freshly made lemonade.

Herman walked up to my father and shook his hand firmly, "Mr. Cole, Sir, it has been a pleasure to have met you and your family. I surely appreciate all the hospitality you have shown me since first we met. I will never forget you, Sir."

I had to admit it, for a ten year old cowboy, he sure knew how to impress.

I was surprised by the quiet, emotion-filled response my father returned. "Son," he said pausing for a moment and searching for the right words, "let me say, if I had been blessed with a boy child, I would have hoped him to be just like you. It has been our pleasure, Herman, to have you in our home and likewise we will always remember you."

Herman then turned a steady eye on Mamma. He continued, but with a shaky voice, "Ma'am, you certainly know how to cook a meal, and I'm sure I will never eat as good a strawberry shortcake as I have had at your table. Thank-you, Mrs. Cole."

TERESA LEE

Mamma's eyes teared up as she hugged her mini Matt Dillon for the last time. She was too emotional to say anything back and still keep from crying. She didn't want to make things worse.

Finally it was our turn. A ten-year-old cowboy, with fancy shirts and a ten gallon hat, turned his gaze on my sisters and me as we stood in a little covey together in the middle of our living room floor. Our own eyes were brimming with tears as we stood watching the good-byes. Then Herman Greene walked right up to Jackie and then to me and kissed us each on the cheek. He never acted one bit ruffled or embarrassed. It was just the most natural way of saying good-bye that he knew, like the farewells you'd get from a cousin or a brother. He bent down and hugged my little sisters and kissed each one on the top of the head. Cathy started crying and hugged his leg. We all felt like crying, too, but instead we started laughing as my baby sister clung to his leg like a monkey to a tree. Even Herman had to smile at her effort in not letting go. And then, there was nothing more to be said except the thing we had avoided most...

"I sure will miss y'all," he whispered with a weak smile. Then he added, "I must hold on to the idea that we will see each other again, so I'll not be saying a proper good-bye just now if you don't mind." No one minded even a little bit.

I sure hoped we would see each other again someday. Until then, I would be praying for God's care over the first real cowboy I ever knew. We promised that we'd write and send pictures. We kept that promise for a long time. Here's a picture of Herman that he sent in one of his letters: A ten-year-old cowboy who wore the fanciest shirts I had ever seen, used manners fit for a king, had a slightly crooked nose and was blessed with hair the color of Wonder Bread toasted just right. I would always remember our Alberquerque cowboy and crawdad king.

TERESA LEE

Chapter Twenty-Three

No Going Back

Your best friend can be better than family in some ways, because you get to choose. There is little or no say in who gets to be family. Friends are people you make a choice about; like whether time is spent with them, or time is spent away from them.

I appreciated those friends who always shared a smile. The special ones who genuinely cared how you felt or what you thought. Still, there was only one Mary Francis. Even though she sometimes tried my patience (and me hers) we always stuck together.

The long trek back to Michigan didn't seem nearly as long as the going to New Mexico. Mamma and Daddy planned a return trip that would be both entertaining and educational. Our visit to The Grand Canyon was of course spectacular, but for me the most memorable thing was meeting Chief Geronimo's grandson, Chief Deerfoot, at the visitor center in the Grand Canyon National Park. He was dressed in buckskin pants with fringe running down the sides. His shirt was a long, striped tunic belted at the waist with porcupine quills hand sewn on the front to form circles and stars that made it look genuinely Native American indeed. He wore his long dark hair braided and secured with a band that ran across his forehead and was tied on the side. Feathers and beads hung down over one ear secured with a strip of buckskin cord at the end of the braid. His eyes were dark and sleepy looking, almost droopy. My sisters and I kept our distance and just watched as other visitors talked with him quietly. My dad seemed fascinated by this flesh and blood descendant of the notorious, Geronimo. They spoke together for some minutes. This grandson of Geronimo's was friendly, though he listened more than he talked. When he did talk, he spoke softly and slowly.

Chief Geronimo was a famous Native American Chieftain that had earned a reputation for being a great leader of his people. His grandson was old too, not young like Mom and Dad. So, I figured that Geronimo himself had already been passed away for fifty years or longer by 1959.

While my sisters and I sat quietly on a stone bench soaking up this moment of importance, a short, stocky woman with a head of black hair cut in a bowl style brought a glass of water to Chief Deerfoot. Her long dark green skirt was covered to her hips with a cranberry colored tunic. The colors reminded me of Christmas. A silver chain belt was around her waist. It was connected together every six inches or more with big, square-shaped silver flowers that reflected the sun like a mirror. A long linked chain hung down from her waist almost to her knees. Feathers and shells were tied to the end of the chain. As she walked along the path, her belt sounded like Grandma Cole's garden wind chime when the breeze made it ting-a-ling ever so softly.

TERESA LEE

We had encountered many Native American people as we made our way across the United States. While we lived in New Mexico we got to enjoy the Southwest Indian Festival held nearby. I was captivated by the music they played on strange instruments, the songs they sang and chanted, the rhythms of their dances. I know for sure that was when my great interest in studying Native American Cultures began. Every school report that I was assigned from fifth grade on, usually centered on Indian Culture in the United States.

The Corn Palace in Utah was another stop we made that was worth remembering. The mosaics displayed there were made of corn and other naturally grown crops. The colors were beautiful and the pictures that were created through the mosaic artistry were amazing. Huge walls covered with corn of different colors and shapes, together with other grains grown in the region, made a storybook history of the Native American Cultures living in that part of the country. We also visited: Carlsbad Caverns (a huge network of naturally occurring underground caves in the Southwest of Texas), the hideout of Jesse James and his brother, Frank (famous bank robbers from the 1800s), The Badlands, The Painted Desert. We saw Mt. Rushmore, where gigantic heads of four of our U.S. Presidents have been chiseled out of rock on the side of a mountain.

All were places of interest that Mamma and Dad were determined for us to see. At each special stop, I sent a postcard to Herman and Mary Francis. I told each of them the news, what we had been seeing, and how missed they were by all of us. It all added up to a lengthy return back to Michigan, but one that Jackie and I would long remember, and which also made us better traveled than most other kids our age.

Our reunions in Michigan came at last, not only with Grandpas and Grandmas, cousins, and friends, but with our old neighborhood gang as well. Everyone knew, compliments of Mary Francis, that even though we were back, things were still going to be different. We would be living in a town down the road about twelve miles from Dartmouth Drive. Still, it was good to realize that we could easily visit all the friends and family we had left four long months ago. For Mary Francis and me, slumber parties were back in the mix, and days spent at each other's houses were going to be something to look forward to again. We were starting over. Things were different now, and would never be exactly the same. We were taking what we could get and being happy with it!!

The very first time we came back to the old neighborhood, everyone seemed to know that we were coming. Mrs. Carson had planned a coffee hour for Mamma with neighborhood friends. All the moms belonging to our little gang were there to welcome us back. Ruth had taken the day off from work at the drugstore and was serving coffee and cakes to the ladies, with cookies and lemonade for the kids. Neighbors were coming like a steady stream, for a drop-in visit. The moms were so glad to see Mamma again. That neighborly caring and concern was like old times. The doors were open once again. The coffee was brewing, and those familiar yummy smells were drifting across autumn breezes, fed by the start of another changing season. The smiles were generously passed around by everyone, young and old alike. We were home again, where we belonged. It was the best of days!

All of the kids in the neighborhood cheered and laughed, hollered and yelled with happiness that couldn't be ignored. We greeted each other with joyous abandon at our good fortune of being reunited.

TERESA LEE

It was a great day with all of us being together once more. Our first priority of business was to head for Saddle Canyon so that I could see our forts again. I needed to discover for myself what had or had not been done since I left. I secretly wondered if things had changed much in four long months. It looked the same, but something was different.

There seemed to be a new unexpected shyness between us as we talked together. We were more aware of being kind and considerate, since this special time back together was not going to last as it had before we moved. No one knew exactly when we'd be seeing each other again. Since were weren't in New Mexico anymore, maybe it wouldn't be months, but it sure wouldn't be every day either. It was as if we were all trying to put on this new idea of moving on, but still wanting life to stay as it had been before we left. All the while, knowing in our hearts that it could never be that way again, not really. With my family living in another town, how could it ever be the same?

I loved seeing everyone and everything so much! It was just as I had dreamed about so many times while we were away; the coming home time when every-thing with the world would be right again. A huge lump came to my throat when we drove up to Carson's house. Immediately we all looked next door. There sat our little house that we had loved so well. It looked dif-ferent. How could it have changed in four months? I was fighting that lump in my throat and defying the tears to come to my eyes. It looked so small compared to the two story, rambling house with eleven rooms, that had belonged to my great-grandparents and for two weeks now, we had come to call home. I thought about the long dark hall in the upstairs of the place that was now our house. The scary door at the end of that hall led to the walk-in attic where bats and squirrels sometimes lived. All my sisters and I agreed, "CREEPY!" Everything about it was so very strange to us.

The house that Daddy had built for us at 502 Dartmouth Drive, looked somehow sad, and lonely as if its heart was missing **us** as much as we were missing being there. Someone else lived there now. It would never be our house again. I thought about the days of bliss living with my family, just next door to Mary Francis. I imagined how the laughter of our family had gotten stuck in the many little cracks and crannies of the house; all the while waiting quietly for the right moment. Then softly, in the stillness of a night, our laughter might come floating out; drifting about the rooms, filling our house again with happiness, for the new strangers to hear. I liked pretending that the little house had found a way to tell them "I don't belong to you." I felt like someone had died; someone that I loved very much. The tears came to my eyes, despite my not wanting them. Mamma's eyes watered up, too. It all became so clear to me, in those moments of looking at our forlorn little six-room house on Dartmouth Drive. I sensed the subtle changes in my friends and our Saddle Canyon paradise. I sadly realized that you can never really go back. You can only go on.

TERESA LEE

Chapter Twenty-Four

Orchard Street

The place where we came to live had belonged to my great grandparents. The house was nearing a hundred years old. It was a big house, very big. It had been used as a boarding house years before when my great grandparents were much younger. With Great Grandpa's big garden in the back, his chicken yard, and his small fruit tree orchard, the property had taken up half of a block. Great-grandpa had died from the hiccups two years before we moved to New Mexico. Great-grandma, Hattie Sanborn Dean, had died three years before my great grandfather. No one had lived in their house since then. Everything still sat just as it had on the day John Dean died.

It was the huge century-old trees that lined the streets in town that made the whole place look like a picture postcard of Small Town America. I yearned for the familiar surroundings of Railroad Town, yet I couldn't help but be impressed by the hundreds of huge old oaks and maples that shared their shade each day. On hot days the gigantic, ancient trees provided comfort from the sun as people walked along on their way to wherever they happened to be going. In the old neighborhood on Dartmouth Drive, there had been few trees of any size left standing. The whole neighborhood was created from huge tracts of land being cleared for development. If you wanted a tree in your yard, it was your job to plant one. Daddy had done just that, and a small red maple had grown much bigger in the five years we had lived there.

The first two weeks back from New Mexico, Daddy and Mamma had driven around to many towns looking to see if there was another place they liked better for settling down and making a new start. They agreed on not being too far away from other family. We had already been through that experience! Mamma liked the idea of keeping the house of my great grandparents in the family. It was just sitting there empty and not being used. Daddy was definitely in the right business for making the changes to the house that Mamma would be wanting. We all agreed that it was a pretty town with friendly people, and lots of kids to play with. So happily, Grandpa Jackson and Daddy struck a deal that both could live with, shaking hands to seal the agreement. For our family of six, it seemed the right fit and the right place for us to settle down.

One Twenty-Eight East Orchard Street had been one of the only boarding houses in town. An open, oak-trimmed, spindled staircase greeted you as you opened the front door. What a grand staircase it was! It had two flights of steps going up. Five steps on the bottom with a big landing in the middle and then another flight of nine steps which led the way to four bedrooms and a bathroom upstairs. Downstairs was a huge dining room in the middle of the house, located directly off from a roomy kitchen on the South end and back of the house. From the dining room table, you could look out of a large window onto a tree lined street. The window had a window seat and set of drawers beneath it. An old player piano sat against the far wall where Great-grandpa Dean had played and entertained the boarders after Sunday dinner was served. A huge wooden oak sideboard, like a china cabinet, was stationed on the wall between the bathroom door and the bedroom door on the first floor. Great-grandma stored her china dishes there and served food for the household meals from that spot.

In the kitchen, we liked the old-fashioned woodstove with two ovens. One oven above the hot plates and one below, were used for cooking, baking, and keeping the kitchen warm in the winter. Out the back door and two steps down just off from the kitchen, was a rickety old covered porch attached to the back of the house. That's where the split wood was neatly stacked for easy access to help fuel the wood stove. My sisters and I hated that dark old walk-through shed. It was full of spiders and mice. Great-grandpa had kept a cat to keep the mouse population in check. YUK!! With no pets at our house, there was sure to be an explosion of four-legged rodents in no time!

There was a real, working, iron hand-pump that brought water into the long, low, white porcelain sink. About once a day you actually had to pour water into the top to prime it. Great-grandma and Great-grandpa Dean used it for washing dirty hands and dishes. It also served as the cleaning center for the many fruits and vegetables that came from Great-grandpa's garden. The produce used to round out the menus, my great-grandparents served up for their boarders, every day of the week.

A sitting room and living room were on opposite sides of the house across the front. A long narrow open walkway ran the full length of the house from the front door to the back, so that boarders could get to the different areas of the house easily. The doors to my great-grandparents' bedroom and one small bathroom were off from the dining room and living room, and located on the west side of the house. When you walked through the front door, you were faced with four walls papered with huge burgundy colored feathers and dark area rugs covering the shiny wooden floors.

Great-grandpa Dean never liked Great-grandma's choice of wall cover and said it looked like, "Funeral home wallpaper." *What exactly was that supposed to mean? No clue.* Why he said that I never knew, but Mamma thought maybe it was on account of him not caring one whit for funeral homes. He never went to funerals, except to Great-grandma's, his very own wife's funeral, and only because my grandma made him. John Dean could be a stubborn man, and he always said he wasn't going to have a funeral for himself, but he did. Grandma Jackson also saw to that!

Whatever the reason, we all knew (without a doubt) that it wasn't Mamma's style either. The "funeral home" wallpaper would be one of the first things to go! Mamma had that paper down and the walls repainted a much brighter, light beige, color within three months of us moving there. As usual, Grandpa and Grandma Jackson came to help every chance they got. I think they liked watching the house come to life. Mamma and Grandma made new curtains for the whole house, and it was looking more like home every day. The gloominess was lifting.

Daddy gutted and cleaned out the old chicken coop on the back corner of the lot. He made it into a playhouse for his four little girls. My sisters and I were liking our new home better each week that passed. The front door of the house was massive. A heavy wooden, beveled glass, old fashioned, windowed door, with a big gold oval-shaped door knob on both sides. The door opened out onto a very large circular-shaped porch which adorned the front of the house. Five massive round pillars supported the porch roof, which covered an area where rocking chairs, braided rugs and planters all made for a most comfortable resting place. You could sit and watch the world go by, as you rocked away the time of day or night. All of it was lovely to say the least, but so big, so dark, and so different.

Our new street had huge old trees up and down each side for as far as you could see. In our side yard alone we had four big red and silver maples that would provide us with hours of raking and fun every year when autumn rolled around. The one in the backyard was more than three feet around the trunk. Jackie and I measured it one day with Great-grandma's sewing tape that had been left in her mending basket. That was one old tree! We wondered just how old it was and when it had been planted. It probably could have bragged more years older than my Great-grandpa Dean, and he was OLD!

The houses on either side of us, directly across the street, were occupied by old people, but it didn't take long for us to get acquainted with several families with kids that lived close by. There were two families that had nothing but boys! The Dumars had five older boys. The Southwicks had four boys. Three of the boys were just about our ages. Donnie, Tim and Paul all fit right in to our age brackets. Jeff was older and hung out with the Dumar boys. Why couldn't all these boy neighbors have been girls? If they had been girls, maybe both families wouldn't have already known my Great-grandpa Dean quite so well!

Great-grandpa had his very own drawer full of their baseballs stashed away under the dining room window-seat. He hid them there from times when the neighbor boys had hit or thrown their baseballs accidentally into his yard. It wasn't a secret that John Dean could be downright ornery and on the stubborn side. It was true, we always seemed to get stuck with an overabundance of boys living right in our backyard, but even I had to admit that taking baseballs and keeping them was grouchy.

After a few weeks of living in our new place, Daddy made a point of emptying those window-seat drawers full of baseballs and giving back a good number of them to their rightful owners. I think my Grandma J. liked the whole idea of my dad doing that, because she said to him, "That Pa, he was one stinker taking those baseballs away from those kids. I told him time and again to give those balls back! But, No Sir! I guess **we** showed him!" Daddy said he didn't know where the **WE** came from, but everyone laughed.

Our new town provided nearly everything we needed. Three families in town ran small family-owned grocery stores. In addition, within easy walking distance of the downtown area, we had a stately looking bank building, a drugstore, a clothing store, a fine jewelry store, a movie theater, a post office, a small library, a large and regionally famous furniture store and, as in every small town, a funeral home. A main trucking artery, running north and south through our state, coursed right through the middle of town, our Main Street. Two railroad crossings, one across Main Street and the other across Madison Street, split the whole town into North and South mailing addresses.

The elementary school was just one block east off from Main Street and two blocks north of the railroad tracks. It was a two story brick school that held classes for kindergarten through sixth grade. There was more than one classroom for each grade. Homemade

TERESA LEE

hot lunches were served at school five days a week. The junior high school and high school were housed together in a different building, a few blocks away. The elementary school in town used to hold kindergarten through twelfth grade until the new school was built. Mamma and Daddy liked that there was a new school here. It showed that the town's people and those living round about cared about education, just like my parents did. Jackie, Christie and I would be starting in just a few days.

The elementary school had two enormous cylindrical slides running off the back of the building. They looked like metal hamster tubes and were used for fire escapes in the case of a fire emergency. A metal fire escape stairway going down from the second floor hallway ran down the outside on the front of the building near the main entrance to the school office. Jackie and I hoped that we never had to use that route, because it looked pretty shaky! Jackie also fussed about ever having to go down that metal circular fire escape slide, because she didn't even like going down the giant slide in the park when she could see where she was going! This would be a dark, blind ride all the way to the bottom! We were already nervous about starting in a new school, and that was not helping.

Besides the fire escape issues looming, the worst part was that we wouldn't know anyone. We hadn't even had the summer to get to know new friends. My sisters and I had met maybe a handful of kids in our immediate neighborhood. They probably wouldn't even be in our class. School had already started. We had only been living in my great-grandparents' house for a week. How many kids can you get to know in one short week? Mamma and Daddy, with us in tow, went and registered for school on Friday. We would be starting on Monday morning bright and early. My stomach was in a constant state of upset. I needed Mary Francis to do my talking! Moving to a new school was definitely not anything near fun!

It was early fall and our windows were still open at night because the autumn chill was not yet frosting the yards and roofs. At bedtime, in the room Jackie and I shared together, I could hear the familiar whistles of the train engines as they passed in the night. That sound brought me comfort, knowing that it all was still there just as before, and I was only hearing it in a different place. Trains ran through this town daily from East to West, but nowhere near the number we had come to expect as they came roaring in from all four compass points when we still called ourselves Railroaders.

Now we were Ramblers. What did that even mean? What kind of team name was that for a town in Michigan? In our county we had school teams named the Railroaders, the Wolf Pack, the Trojans, the Cavaliers, the Eagles, the Indians and the Orioles. At least those names all made some sort of sense or connection to something else. After I figured out that a Rambler was some sort of car, I still had to ask "So what does that have to do with school teams and activities?" Neither daddy nor Mamma had the slightest idea. Mamma had been a Railroader. Daddy had been an Eagle. Those both were great team names that stood for something important! I settled with the fact that I would have to be content knowing; cars were built in our state, and a Rambler was the make of a car, so it must fit just fine. I sure didn't want to listen to any teasing from my Railroader friends because now I was some silly Rambler person, and had no clear idea just where I got my team name. I was sure Mary Francis would not overlook that fact!

In truth, Mr. Dumar, our neighbor who was the father of five boys and one of the teachers and coaches at the high school, cleared that mystery up for us. One Sunday afternoon, when everyone was out in their yards, Dad asked the very same question that I had put to him at breakfast one morning. Mr. Dumar shared the story about how the school's early basketball teams didn't have a proper gym floor on which to host an official game. The team had to travel around to other schools just to compete. So, the name Ramblers was adopted to signify our rambling around from place to place just to get a game. I knew he must have the truth of it, because he had lived there his entire life and was a true Rambler! Daddy said that Mr. Harold Dumar had been a three sport standout in his day. That meant he had been real good at playing sports and being a Rambler.

Actually, I thought that the red and gray mascot car, adopted many years after the team name was chosen, was very cool! It even backfired now and then when it was driven in a parade or onto the football field, which always made everyone jump! My new school song was the same as the popular university fight song "On Wisconsin". It had a great tune and was easy to sing along with, so all in all it could have been much worse. My heart and head was fighting against being anything other than a Railroader. It was all just going to take some getting used to by everyone in our family. We were all ready to take on the challenge because it was so good to be home in Michigan once again, and this time to stay!

Chapter Twenty-Five

New School... New Friends

Many people come and go in your life, but only a very few remain to become a best friend. One thing is for certain, the day when that special friend is discovered will be one of the best days of your life. The day you find one of those friendships of a lifetime, will be a day that keeps on giving. If you are lucky, you will feel the worth of it until you are old and gray.

The first day of school came as promised. Dad was going to take us to school on the first morning. Mamma stayed home with little Cathy. My littlest sister would be starting school next year as a kindergartner. Dad parked the car across the street from the school under a huge oak tree that shaded the car. I took Christie by the hand. She was whimpering softly.

I was talking to her with encouraging words, so as to ease her heart and mind,

"Now you are going to love your teacher! Remember how nice she was when you met her last week? Mamma says she is just the best! Besides that, Mrs.

Toby is a good friend of Grandma's so you're sure to be one of her favorites. As soon as school is out, I will come right to your classroom to get you. Wait for me there. Jackie and I will both come and we will all walk home together." Christie looked up into Daddy's eyes with tears clinging to her eye lashes.

She reached out to take his hand. "Daddy, I want to go home and see Mamma. I don't like the lunch here." she protested.

"O.K., Willie, this is the deal. We are going to go to your classroom. You are going to say 'Good Morning, Mrs. Toby,' with your very best big girl manners. Then you are going to have a great first day in Second Grade and eat every bit of the lunch your Mamma packed you." With a big smile, he handed her a brand new lunch pail. Mamma's surprise for the first day of school. Her eyes immediately lit up like a Christmas tree. "Now be my big girl and show us how it's done!" he concluded.

Christie always loved a challenge and she took this one on full strength. We all loved to make our Daddy happy. Her eyes sparkled at the new shiny lunch pail Daddy held out for her. Christie clamped her fingers around the handle of her new Minnie Mouse lunch pail very tightly, took a deep breath, stood up straight and led Daddy across the street, with Jackie and me following on their heels. We dropped her off in a flash. Not one tear was shed. She made Daddy so proud. *If she could do it, so could I!*

Daddy had forgotten some papers the school secretary had to have to prove we had our vaccinations. We couldn't be at school without having them first filed. So back to the car Daddy, Jackie and I all went to retrieve the forgotten items. We turned away from the car and started up the sidewalk to the front door of the school. Jackie and I looked up at a movement that

TERESA LEE

caught our eye from the second story windows facing out at the front lawn of the building. About nine or ten kids were lined up at the windows staring at us as we walked up the long sidewalk to enter our new school.

"Looks like a welcoming committee," Daddy said with a laugh.

Personally I didn't think it was quite that funny. *Who were all those kids staring at us like we were from* "The Twilight Zone?" My stomach was doing flips and I felt sick. Jackie's ears were flaming red and I knew she was scared. Her ears always turned red when she was upset or scared. You couldn't help but notice those red ears with her blonde hair pulled so tightly into the one long braid that hung down to the middle of her back. I was glad my hair was short and covered up my ears. I wasn't going to say one word about her red ears. She probably would have burst into tears. *I sure felt like it! If anyone teased her about her red ears they would be sorry!*

I was ever so grateful that Mamma had taken special care to let us wear our freshly ironed new dresses to school. I wore my pink and white gingham checked dress with the tiny lace trim around the cap sleeves and collar. A matching wide sash went around my waist and tied in a big bow at the back. Jackie had on her blue and white plaid dress with the white collar. The attached white apron went around her waist, fastened with pretty blue buttons in the front. It too, tied in the back with a big white bow. That dress made her eyes look like the prettiest blue of the ocean.

As we approached Jackie's classroom, the door opened. A wide-eyed boy exited the room holding a bathroom pass on a chain. He smiled and quickly passed by. I could see Jackie's chin quivering, and her ears were not one bit less red.

"Wait for your sister after school. She will come for you first and then the two of you go and get Willie from her class." Daddy finished as he tipped up her chin and gave her a kiss on the cheek. *Same routine.* "Have a good day, mind your teachers and enjoy your lunch! School will be over before you can count to five hundred!" *That's not true!*

"No it won't," Jackie replied with a sad pout.

Jackie's teacher came to the door at Daddy's knock. She greeted us all with a big smile and warm welcome. Jackie strained to look back at us over her shoulder as she was led off to greet her new classmates and have her fourth grade school year begin. *Her ears were still flaming red.*

Our last stop was my classroom door. I was wishing so much that I was home with Mamma and little Cathy. I knew just how Christie felt, but if she could do it in second grade, I certainly could do it in fifth! The door opened again at my father's soft rap. Mrs. Larkin appeared at the door in a matter of seconds. She opened the door wide, and I could feel all sets of eyes in that room directed squarely on me. Daddy was standing with his hand on my back. Inside my head I was screaming: *Daddy, don't leave me alone here, PLEASE!*

"Well, Mr. Cole, isn't it? This must be your daughter, Terry? We are so glad to have you join our class, my dear. I have a desk all set up for you, and I understand that you live right next door to Kathy Gleason." Mrs. Larkin turned and pointed out Kathy Gleason, who stood up with an easy smile and a small wave.

She continued, "I put your desks together so that Kathy can help you get used to how things work around here. She'll be your new best friend for a few days until you get more comfortable. We all will have

228   TERESA LEE

a fine year of learning together." Mrs. Larkin finished with as friendly a voice as I had ever heard.

My dad interjected quickly and quietly, "Mrs. Larkin, thank you so much for making all of us feel welcome at the girls' new school. We sure appreciate your concern for their well-being. My wife asked me to say that if there is anything you need during this school year, please feel free to give us a call or send a note along with Terry. She would have come herself, but is at home with our four year old daughter. Terry will pick up her younger sisters every day after school for the walk home. We're mighty grateful for all your help." Daddy finished with a smile and handshake for Mrs. Larkin.

After a quick hug and kiss on the forehead, Daddy turned to go. I grabbed the sleeve of his shirt and held on. I could feel all those sets of eyes burning a hole in my back. I whispered softly with a trembling voice, "I'll see you after school, Daddy. Thanks for our new lunch pails. Tell Mamma I will eat all of my lunch. Tell little Cathy that I will play with her as soon as we get home from school today."

I was desperately trying to think of something, anything else to say to keep him there for just one minute longer. I think Mrs. Larkin knew I was stalling. With a quick nod to my father she then guided me into the classroom, closing the door quietly behind us. Daddy told me later that he waited for a few minutes outside the door to be sure that I would be all right. *I just never could fool Daddy no matter how hard I tried.*

As it all turned out, Christie met Jill, her best friend, that very first day. They sat beside each other for the rest of the school year and for many years to come. *Why were lunches never a point of complaint for Christie after her first day as a Rambler? After all, who could argue against a school menu with the BEST homemade cinnamon rolls ever? We didn't have that at Robert Kerr School. I would remember and make a point of that fact with Mary Francis.*

That was the start to my fifth grade year, and the beginning of a new life in a new place. Leggins didn't exist here. This new beginning had rubbed out that name at last. It was a welcomed change. I didn't believe that I would ever miss that nickname. I made my sisters swear never to tell anyone here about that name. I knew they would keep their promise. They hated seeing their big sister cry!

My teacher was right about one thing. Kathy Gleason was my new best friend that day and for many days and years to come. The best thing of all was that she lived right next door to us, just like Mary Francis! We would have endless days ahead of playing in the old chicken coop between our houses, pajama parties with friends, and shared vacations. But even with all that said, she didn't take one thing away from Mary Francis, and Mary Francis didn't take anything away from her. They were different in many ways, but the same in knowing how to be a special friend. I think Mary Francis knew I needed someone in the place where I had been planted. I sure knew she needed someone, too. So Mary Francis came to spend weekends and Kathy came over to play. I went to Mary's house for sleepovers just the way we had planned. Mary Francis introduced me to Julie Morris, who was one of the new friends Mary Francis had found. We all got along just fine.

Living in any new place has its ups and downs. My sisters and I made many new friends as before, different names, different faces, but in many ways the same. Friends with problems, friends who would always tease, friends who made life more interesting. Fun filled our days in this new place we had come to live. There would always be the Dale Hensleys, going about with a chip on their shoulder; in general, mad at the world. Like Harold Baskey, who loved all the girls, but few loved him back. He once shaved off his eyebrows just to prove a point when one of his heart-throbs gave him back his ring. How Harold ever thought that shaving off his eyebrows would impress a girl, I hadn't the faintest idea!

How about the Ricky Grants who tease and offer up dares to see who might take it. Yep, Billy Carlson, fifth grade, dared me to stick my tongue on the swing-set pole in the middle of January. I couldn't eat any solid food for three whole days after that challenge!

Compassionate caring with friends like Toby Taylor, who had special circumstances? Yes, again. Virginia Nester, sitting directly in front of Jackie during a fire drill slide, came down the escape tube leading from their sixth grade classroom. She had one of her first epileptic seizures when she exited the slide into the schoolyard. All the kids at our school watched over Virginia after that day, especially my sister, Jackie.

Just like my other best friend, Charlie Sinclair, Jr. who shared more than just a bad habit with me, Billy Connor and Tommy Dickerson appreciated the rock collection that my sisters and I had worked so hard to gather and display. They liked the Native American souvenirs that we had carted back with us from our travels out west. Both liked to hear the stories over and over about living in New Mexico, and all the special spots we had visited. My sisters and I loved telling the stories and they seemed to never tire of hearing them.

New faces, new places, new friends came with surprisingly similar circles of life. Strange how things can change, yet stay the same in many ways. Different faces now, but day-to-day life, pretty much a rubber stamp for how people everywhere and at every age manage to get along and count their days of living.

Mary Francis and I had both grown up a bit in those four long months that we were apart. We learned to care more for each other's happiness than we cared about being jealous or selfish regarding new friends. The bond between us would never be broken. Life had to go on and so did we. The best part of all was that we were close enough to see each other whenever we needed. Some people aren't that lucky. We learned that you can find friendship in other places, too. Sometimes when things seem the worst possible, given time most things turn out all right. We both were certain sure that we were blessed to have each other, always. Yep, together we would forever be Leggins and Mary Francis and that would never change. It would always be enough for us.

TERESA LEE

Author's Note

My wish would be that every human being might experience at least once in their lifetime, the pure joy of having a best friend to treasure forever. Truly, this is a blessing which gives in greatest measure. The gift of unconditional friendship can be life changing, character altering, and an intricate part in the well-being of the human soul.

The tales of friendship here span many years. The fun of being friends fills our memories with many stories that others share, too. It was fun. It was maddening. It was friendship made of love and caring, fighting and making up, tears and laughter. It was a treasure map made out of days filled with neighborhood friends and games, pajama parties and picnics, treks to Saddle Canyon and other intriguing destinations. A well-worn trail with points of interest like the snow days when we stayed home from school, birthday parties amid other family celebrations, and summer trips to Canada and Northern Michigan. Mary Francis and I followed the map we created and along the way built a lasting bond that held us together and could lighten up the darkest of days, even many years after it had all started.

Life situations line the pages of the story shared here, and may be similar to ones you have experienced yourself. Relive the laughter. Remember the life lessons the stories share. Always cherish your friends as a gift you'll never outgrow. The spirit of friendship can last a lifetime, even beyond death. True friendship is the blessed source of memorable human interaction expressing selflessness, genuine mutual concern, and unquestioned loyalty. Unfortunately, sometimes best friends enjoy a short journey together here on earth. Tragically, life can deal a blow unexpectedly, and it all can end much too soon.

Our remembrances, of dear friends, remain their legacy of love. Cherishing the memories continues to polish the golden treasure of friendship:

Shared moments beyond price,

Loyalties that stand the test of time,

Genuine joy in recalling the laughter,

Wisdom gained from walking
through life together,

Understanding that love
can be unconditional.

All this and more has filled our treasure chest
of friendship.

We remain.........Best Friends, Forever Friends.............still.

TERESA LEE

Post Note

Mary Francis Carson passed away in Connecticut on August 27, 2011 far from where we grew up together. The local newspaper published a nice article that shared things she had accomplished during her life. It didn't come close to telling the whole story of Mary Francis Carson (1949-2011) or what the dash between her years of life included. She remains and will always be one of my few forever and ever best friends.

I can finally smile in the remembering.

About the Author

Teresa Lee has been an educator of children for more than thirty years. "Leggins" is her second published children's chapter book. Her first published book, "Boxcar Joe," was released in December 2013.

The author delights in sharing her stories with former students and friends of all ages. Teresa Lee's stories blend realistic fiction with historical fiction and teach life lessons that readers at any age may embrace. Sharing quality literature with young people has always been a priority. Inspiration comes from living life and experiences that enrich our spirits.

Teresa lives with her husband in the country near Perry, Michigan. She and her family love spending time together whenever possible.

Teresa believes, "Everyone has a fascinating story waiting to be told. No one else can share your story in quite the same way as you. Celebrate those special moments and write your experiences, because you just never know when one of those stories might become a best seller!"

About the Illustrator

Jann Johnson Lardie always wanted to be an artist. However, the loving demands of life, family and career, took her away from the pursuit of art. Upon retirement, she jumped whole-heartedly back into the world of art by exploring pottery, ceramic sculpture, painting with pastels and monotypes.

In 2011, friend and author, Teresa Lee, asked Jann to illustrate "Boxcar Joe," and subsequently, "Leggins" – adding another fun chapter to her art-filled life.

CPSIA information can be obtained
at www.ICGtesting.com
Printed in the USA
FFOW05n1850250815